# GRAVE DELIGHT

## A MADDIE GRAVES MYSTERY BOOK THREE

### LILY HARPER HART

HARPERHART PUBLICATIONS

Copyright © 2015 by Lily Harper Hart

All rights reserved.

No part of this book may be reproduced in any form or by any electronic or mechanical means, including information storage and retrieval systems, without written permission from the author, except for the use of brief quotations in a book review.

❀ Created with Vellum

## 1. ONE

"I'm not wearing that."

Maddie Graves placed her hands on her narrow waist, her long blonde hair flying as she regarded the tiny black dress her grandmother Maude was holding up.

"You're a young woman, Maddie," Maude said, making a face. "You have a beautiful body. You're going out on a date with the man of your dreams. You should look like you're not Amish."

"This is a perfectly nice dress," Maddie said, holding up a modest blue sheath so her grandmother could study it. "It matches my eyes."

"It's fine," Maude said.

"Thank you." If Maddie thought the argument was over, she was about to get a rude awakening.

"Fine is not how you want to look when you're about to go out with the hottest man in town," Maude said. "Fine is how you want to look when you have a hangover on a Sunday and you don't want the minister to know you were out imbibing until the wee hours on a Saturday night."

"Thank you so much for that visual, Granny," Maddie said, her tone dry. "I don't think I need to wear ... that ... to excite Nick."

Maddie's petal pink lips tipped into a smile at the mention of her boyfriend, Nick Winters. He'd only been her boyfriend for a grand total of two weeks. He'd been her best friend for the better part of her life, though. While most things remained the same between them since the shift in their relationship, a lot of things had changed.

"See, you're having wanton thoughts," Maude said, grinning.

"I am not."

"You are, too," Maude said. "It's written all over your face."

"Don't go there, Granny," Maddie said. "I'm not talking to you about this. I told you that any sex talk was off the table where you and I are concerned. It's just too ... icky."

"If you think sex is icky you're going to have a hard time doing it right," Maude said, nonplussed. "Maybe I should get you a book." She tapped her chin thoughtfully, her steel-gray curls bouncing. "I'll get on the Internet while you're out and get you a book. You're probably going to need pictures, right?"

"Granny, if I find any kind of ... sex book ... in this house I'm going to lock you in your room," Maddie said, her eyes flashing. "I'm not joking."

"I'll make you a deal," Maude said. "If you put this dress on and wear it on your date I won't buy a book."

Maddie was caught. She knew it. *She planned this.* "Fine," Maddie said, snatching the dress from her grandmother. "I know what you did here, though. Don't think I don't."

"What did I do?" Maude was a master at feigning innocence. "I just want you to look your very best when you go out to dinner. Where are you going anyway?"

"Nick is taking me out to that nice seafood restaurant out on the lake," Maddie said. "It's supposed to be beautiful."

"And expensive," Maude said. "I've heard great things about that restaurant. You're going to have a good time."

Maude held Maddie steady as she slipped into the tight black dress. It wasn't even Maddie's. She didn't own anything this slinky. Her friend Christy, a local hairdresser, had dropped off an armful of clothes for another date – with another guy – weeks before. She'd never bothered to reclaim them.

"Oh, I can't wear this," Maddie said, glancing at her reflection in the mirror and yanking on the low neckline in an attempt to pull it up. "My boobs are on display."

"Your boobs are hardly on display," Maude said. "That dress fits you like it was made for you. Nick's going to go crazy when he sees it."

*That was an interesting thought,* Maddie mused. After admitting their love for each other during an emotional confrontation, Nick put a moratorium on sex. He said he wouldn't even consider it for two weeks. He wanted them to get a chance to get to know each other as boyfriend and girlfriend before they got to know each other in the Biblical sense. That moratorium ended tonight – and Maddie found she was incredibly nervous. She was worried the dress would send the wrong message – although she had no idea what that message was.

"I don't want Nick to go crazy," Maddie said. "I just want to have a nice night ... with a nice dinner. He's been busy at work."

As a local Blackstone Bay police officer, Nick was almost always on call. While crime wasn't rampant in the small town, he was often forced to mediate drunken altercations and long held blood feuds between senior citizens. Of course, Maude was often in the middle of the blood feuds so that made things easy when they wanted to spend time together.

In addition to the normal Blackstone Bay shenanigans, the town also played host to two murders in recent months, and the residents were on edge.

"Oh, just suck it up," Maude said. "You finally have everything you've ever wanted. Enjoy it ... and if you take that dress off I'm going to disown you."

Maddie opened her mouth to argue with her grandmother, instead taking an involuntary step back when her mother Olivia popped into view. After spending ten years away from Blackstone Bay on a self-imposed exile, Maddie only recently returned following the death of her mother. So, to be fair, her mother's body wasn't in the room. It was just her soul.

"You look lovely," Olivia said, smiling at her only daughter, as she shimmered next to her.

"Hi, Mom," Maddie said, exhaling shakily. She was still getting used to being able to see through her mother instead of curling up on her lap, but she'd take her any way she could get her.

"Your mother is here?" Maude brightened. "Tell her I said hi."

"She can hear you, Granny," Maddie said.

While a magical "peculiarity" ran through the Graves family's genes, it skipped Maude. She'd never missed being able to see ghosts – or psychic visions – until her only daughter died. Now, every time Olivia popped in for a visit, Maddie saw the yearning on her grandmother's face. It tugged at her heart.

"Tell her I said hi," Olivia said, smiling fondly at the woman she'd lived with for the bulk of her life. "Tell her I love her hair."

"She says hi and she loves your hair," Maddie said.

"Of course she loves my hair," Maude said, patting it. "I look like a super model."

Maddie could think of a few other words, but she wisely let them slide. She ran her hands over the black dress, smoothing it down as she stared at her reflection in the mirror. "You don't think this dress is too ... slutty ... do you?"

"There's nothing slutty about that dress," Olivia said. "In fact, you look like a dream. You look like Nick's dream."

Maddie's cheeks burned under the praise. "I ... ."

"She told you to keep the dress on, didn't she?" Maude asked knowingly.

"She said I look slutty," Maddie lied.

"She did not," Maude said, slapping Maddie's arm lightly. "I may not be able to hear her, but I know she would never say anything of the sort. Don't lie. I don't like it."

"Fine," Maddie said, giving in. "She said I look like a dream."

"You look like Nick's dream," Maude said, smiling.

"That's exactly what Mom said."

"Great minds think alike." Maude stepped closer to Maddie, giving her a brief hug. Affection wasn't ever withheld in the Graves household when Maddie was growing up, but hugs were still a valuable currency. "I love you, Maddie girl."

"I love you, too, Granny," Maddie said. "If someone mistakes me for a prostitute in this dress, though, I'm totally blaming you."

"I'm sure I'll have it coming," Maude said.

**NICK WINTERS** leaned against the wall in the stairwell, smiling as he listened to the conversation a few feet away. He'd let himself into the house with the spare key, never once thinking of knocking. Even before he and Maddie officially became a couple he'd never resorted to knocking. He was part of the family.

While Nick never thought of himself as a depressed individual, the joy he'd experienced over the past two weeks had been nothing short of extraordinary. It turned out the only thing he needed to make his life perfect was the most beautiful blonde in the world. The fact that she just happened to be the best friend he'd ever had was icing on the cake of a very exciting life.

After a few minutes of eavesdropping, Nick began to wonder how he was going to interrupt the conversation without tipping them off that he'd been listening when he shouldn't have been. Nothing in the world could make him break up this conversation, though, especially once Olivia joined the fray.

While Nick couldn't see Olivia, and he'd been angry when Maddie finally admitted her big secret, he was happy Maddie still had a piece of the mother she loved so much to hold on to. After ten years without the woman he loved more than anything, he was willing to embrace her psychic abilities without reservation. He would take Maddie as she was and be proud of everything she could do.

"I still don't know," Maddie said. "I think I should change. Nick should be here any second."

Nick desperately didn't want her to change out of that dress. Just hearing Maddie talk about it practically had him salivating. Even though he'd been the one to put the moratorium on sex, he was ready now. The only problem was that the longer they went without doing the deed the bigger it got in both of their minds. It was time to move forward because he was never going to look back.

Nick jumped when Maddie peered around the wall and glanced down the stairwell. He smiled when he saw her, embarrassed he'd been caught but immediately swept up in how lovely she looked. Her heart-shaped face was perfect, only a hint of makeup highlighting her features. Her long legs were on display thanks to the short dress, and her body was ... wow ... just fantastic. She looked like a vision.

"You look like a dream," Nick said, exhaling heavily. "You look like every dream I've ever had about you."

"Were you listening to us?"

"I would deny it, but I know Olivia is up there," Nick said, pushing himself away from the wall and climbing the steps. "She's the one who told you I was out here, wasn't she?"

"I can't believe you were listening," Maddie said, her face coloring. "I ... what did you hear?"

"I heard you and Maude talking about this dress," Nick said. "And, love, you're not changing your clothes. You look ... amazing."

Maddie relaxed, her shoulders softening. "Are you sure?"

"I've never been more sure of anything in my life, Mad," Nick said, leaning over so he could give her a soft kiss. He was still getting used to being able to do it – and he didn't think he'd ever get enough of it. "Well, that's not entirely true," he amended. "I was more sure that I love you than anything else. This is a close second, though."

"See, how am I supposed to yell at you for eavesdropping when you say things like that?" Maddie asked, her face serious but her eyes sparkling.

"I don't want you to yell," Nick said. "I want you to give me another kiss, and then I want you to get a jacket, and then I want you to let me open my truck door for you and take you out to a great dinner. I don't think yelling has to be a part of anything we do tonight."

*Well, maybe something,* Nick added silently.

"Do you really think I need a jacket?" Maddie asked. "It's so nice out."

"The restaurant is on the lake and I reserved a table on the deck," Nick said. "I'd rather be safe than sorry. Although, if you don't want to take a coat I'll give you mine. That would be the gentlemanly thing to do."

"Oh, no one would ever accuse you of not being a gentleman," Maddie teased, leaning forward and planting her lips on Nick's. After a few moments of heavy kissing, Nick was out of breath when Maddie pulled away.

"That was amazing," Nick said, his dark eyes latching onto Maddie's sea-blue orbs. "I love you."

"I love you, too," Maddie said. "Let me say goodbye to Granny and grab my coat."

Nick watched her turn, smiling when a coat shot out from the hallway behind Maddie. Maude glanced around her granddaughter, grinning when she caught sight of Nick. "It's good you dressed up," Maude said. "You two look great together."

"It's a date," Nick replied. "You dress up for a nice date."

"You dress up good," Maude said. "I won't wait up."

"Don't," Nick said. He held out his hand. "Come on, love. We don't want to keep the night waiting."

Maddie took his hand. "No, we definitely don't."

Whatever happened tonight, they were both ready for it. Finally.

## 2. TWO

"This place is beautiful," Maddie said, turning her face into the breeze so she could gaze out at the placid lake. "What a great view."

"I agree," Nick said, never moving his eyes from Maddie's astounding face.

Maddie rolled her eyes when she realized what he was doing. "You're really laying the charm on thick tonight."

"Is that a problem?"

"No," Maddie said. "I just ... you don't have to do anything special to woo me. You know that, right?"

Nick grinned. "Woo you?"

"You know what I mean."

"I think you've been spending too much time with Maude," Nick said. "I don't know anyone under the age of fifty who uses that word. Or ... well ... my mom actually used that word when she found out I broke up with ... ." Nick broke off, immediately regretting the conversational turn.

When Maddie first returned to Blackstone Bay Nick was involved with a local woman named Cassidy Dunham. Even though Nick knew the relationship wasn't going anywhere – he had a six-month cycle and he stuck to it – Cassidy was ravaged when Nick finally broke up with her.

He still felt guilty, even though he hadn't seen Cassidy in almost two weeks. He was done postponing his happiness, though. "I shouldn't have brought her up," Nick said. "I ... that was stupid."

Maddie waved off the apology. "Nicky, don't do that. Just because we're a couple that doesn't mean we're not friends, too. Tell me what your mother said."

"She said I should bring you flowers when I *woo* you," Nick said, chuckling at the memory. "I was mortified. My mother hasn't given me dating advice since ... well ... ever."

"Why do you think she did it this time?"

"Because she knew I would never date anyone else again," Nick replied, guileless. "This is her last chance to impart motherly advice on my dating life."

Maddie rubbed her burning cheek. "Oh ... I ... ."

"You're so darned cute," Nick said. "Even now, after two weeks and constant proclamations of love, you still seem surprised that I mean it."

"I just never thought it would really happen," Maddie said. "I spent years loving you from afar ... and then pining for you from really far away. It's like a dream come true."

Nick reached across the table and captured Maddie's hand, rubbing his thumb over the ridge of her knuckles softly. "It was my dream, too, Mad," he said. "I was just as miserable without you as you were without me."

"Except I was the one who made us miserable by running away," Maddie said.

"I don't want to talk about that again," Nick said, internally sighing. In an attempt to keep her psychic abilities hidden from him, Maddie attended college in downstate Michigan and stopped taking his phone calls, essentially breaking his heart. After the truth came out, he'd made a decision to forgive her because he understood her fear. It was unfounded – there was nothing in this world that could ever make him stop loving her – but he understood it.

"I know," Maddie said, shaking herself out of her reverie. "I shouldn't have brought it up."

"Let's start over," Nick said, smiling broadly. "How was your day, love?"

Maddie giggled. "Well, I did tarot readings for two teenagers, I fought with Granny about the flask she has hidden in the garage, and I had lunch with Christy."

"Oh, wow, that's a busy day," Nick said. "Was there anything off about the readings?"

Maddie was known to uncover a murder – or two – before they happened thanks to her job running her mother's former magic store. When Maddie started shaking her head, Nick couldn't help but let loose with a relieved sigh.

"They were normal," Maddie said. "They were more interested in finding out if they had a chance with the guys from One Direction."

"What's that?"

"It's a band."

"I've never heard of it," Nick said. "Are they new?"

"And British."

"What about the flask?" Nick asked. "What was in it?"

"Whiskey."

"Did you taste it?"

"Um ... maybe," Maddie admitted. "It was hot this afternoon and Granny gives me a headache when she's on a tear."

"Why is she on a tear?" Nick asked, leaning back in his chair and relaxing. "What's got her going now?"

"What always has her going?"

"Harriet Proctor," Nick said, referring to Maude's lifelong nemesis – who just happened to be the grandmother of Maddie's lifelong nemesis, Marla Proctor.

"Yeah, she's still trying to get into the Pink Ladies," Maddie replied. The Pink Ladies was the social group Maude belonged to. From what Maddie could tell, all they did was sit around and play cards while drinking whiskey-laden tea. It still kept her grandmother busy, so she was willing to put up with it.

"I love your grandmother," Nick said. "She's always up to something."

"She's funny," Maddie agreed. "What did you do today?"

"I filled out paperwork and daydreamed about our date," Nick replied, winking.

"Oh, you're so charming and handsome. I can't believe you're all mine," Maddie said, leaning over the table so she could give Nick a soft kiss.

"I *am* all yours," Nick said. "Forever."

"I'M glad you suggested taking a walk before we head back to town," Maddie said, stretching her arms out as she dug her bare toes into the wet sand. "I love a beach at night."

"I do, too," Nick said, watching Maddie play in the sand. She'd always been an "outdoor" girl, and that was only one of the things he loved about her. As teenagers, they spent hours racing through the woods and playing in the small lake behind Maddie's house. Nick would catch turtles for her and she would name them before releasing them. Then she would find a Petoskey stone and give it to him, a whisper of luck on her lips as she pressed it into his hand. He had an entire box of them. He'd never give them up.

Even as the memory pushed to the forefront, Nick fingered the small statue in his pocket. Maddie bought it for him right before he professed his love. It was shaped like a turtle and made out of Petoskey stones. He carried it with him constantly now. It was a reminder of her; a reminder of the love he refused to live without ever again.

"What are you thinking about?" Maddie asked, fixing him with a quizzical look.

"Nothing," Nick said, shaking his head. "Why?"

"You went someplace else."

"I really didn't," Nick said. "I was just thinking about all the time we've spent together by water."

"You're so sappy, Nicky."

"You make me sappy," Nick said, reaching for her and snagging her around the waist so he could twirl her around. Her long legs, mostly bare thanks to the short dress, fanned out as he swung her around. "You make me happy."

Nick pulled Maddie flush against his chest and kissed her, keeping one hand around her waist and trailing the other up her lithe back until it finally lodged in the long flaxen locks he loved to touch.

The couple made out for what felt like forever, and when they finally pulled their lips from one another Nick snuggled Maddie close with a contented sigh.

"You make me happy, too," Maddie whispered.

"I'm glad," Nick said. "I don't like it when you're sad."

Nick pressed his eyes shut, swaying slightly in the night breeze as he held Maddie. After a few minutes, Maddie moved her head from Nick's shoulder.

"We should go," Maddie said.

Nick was surprised with the abrupt shift in the conversation. "What's wrong? Do you feel sick? Was it the seafood? You inhaled that crab like you haven't eaten in weeks."

Maddie pursed her lips, embarrassed. "I was hungry. I ... that's not what I was talking about."

"Oh," Nick said, relieved. "What were you talking about?"

Maddie shrugged, averting her gaze. "Nothing. I just thought ... um ... never mind."

Nick tilted his head to the side, considering. It took him a few moments, but he finally realized what Maddie was referring to. "Did you want to go to my place?" Nick asked, hope welling in his chest.

"I just want to be with you," Maddie said, her voice soft. "It would probably be safer to spend the night at your place tonight, though."

Nick couldn't hide the smile playing at the corner of his mouth. "A night away from Maude is probably a good idea."

Even though they hadn't made love yet, they'd spent every night since declaring their feelings in the same bed. Most of those nights were at Maddie's house because she was reluctant to leave Maude to her own devices for too long, but they weren't going to need an audience for the next step.

"I guess it's good you moved some clothes to my house," Nick said, brushing his lips against her cheek. "As much as I love that dress, you're going to want something comfortable to wear tomorrow."

"Why is that?"

"Because ... ." Now Nick was the one struggling with embarrassment. "Because I always want you to be comfortable with me."

"I could never be comfortable with anyone else," Maddie said.

This time the kiss they shared was more urgent, a promise of a lifetime landing on their lips.

"I need to grab my shoes," Maddie said, finally pulling away.

"I could carry you and you could abandon the shoes," Nick offered.

"I want to feel the sand on my toes while we walk back," Maddie said. "I want to remember everything about tonight."

"I want to remember everything about this life, Mad," Nick said. "Grab your shoes."

Maddie's smile was contagious as she searched the dark sand for her shoes. "Do you remember where I kicked them off?"

"I think it was over by those rocks," Nick said, leaning over so he could scoop up his own shoes. "Hurry up. I'm starting to feel desperate."

"You were the one who put the moratorium on sex," Maddie reminded him.

"Don't remind me," Nick said. "I've cursed my stupidity every day for the past two weeks."

Maddie stilled. "Why didn't you say something?"

Nick sighed. "I'm not sorry we waited," he said. "This has been the best two weeks of my life. I didn't want you always tensing up when I touched you. I wanted you to get comfortable with me before ... this."

"Nicky, I've never been more comfortable with anyone in my entire life."

"This is still a big step for us," Nick said. "There's never going to be someone else for me, Maddie. There never was."

"Is my six-month clock going to start ticking now?" She was joking, but there was a serious tint to her eyes.

"Maddie, don't ever think that," Nick said. "The only reason I dated on a six-month cycle before was because I couldn't have you."

"I know," Maddie said, immediately regretting her words. "I ... that was a stupid thing to say."

"I don't want you ever to doubt that you're my everything," Nick said. "You're not my right now. You're my forever."

"Oh, Nicky." Hot tears flooded her eyes.

"Don't you dare start crying," Nick ordered, extending a finger. "I can't take it. Find your shoes. I'm ready to take you home."

"Me, too," Maddie said, gracing him with a blinding smile. "I really do love you, Nicky."

"I really love you, too."

Maddie returned to her shoe search, the hot fantasies she'd been trying to tamp down for the past two weeks pushing to the forefront of her brain. She was so lost in her reverie she was only half paying attention when her eyes landed on a shoe. She already had it in her hand when she realized it wasn't hers.

Maddie shifted her gaze back down to the sand, narrowing her eyes as she tried to peer into the misty expanse. When she realized what she was looking at – that the shoe had an owner and she was spread eagle on the beach – Maddie's heart caught in her throat.

She opened her mouth to call to Nick, but no sound would come out. Instead, a timid squeak escaped and Nick was at her side within seconds. "What's wrong, love?"

Maddie couldn't do anything but point. When Nick's eyes found what Maddie was gesturing toward his heart dropped. Tonight was not going to be their night after all. It seemed death was visiting Blackstone Bay again, and this time the victim was young and ... brutalized.

"Come here, Maddie," Nick murmured, tugging her to him as he pulled his cell phone out of his pocket. "Don't look, love. Don't look."

## 3. THREE

"You look rough."

Christy Ford sipped from her coffee mug as Maddie shuffled into the kitchen the next morning. After being friendly acquaintances in high school, Maddie and Christy struck up a fast friendship upon Maddie's return to Blackstone Bay. Christy enjoyed dragging Maddie out of her shell – and Maddie enjoyed letting her. It was a beneficial arrangement for both of them.

Maddie ran a hand through her long hair and fixed Christy with a rueful look. "You're making the work I've been doing on my self-esteem so much easier. Thank you."

Christy grinned. "Actually, I think I am. You just said something sarcastic. I wasn't sure if you knew what sarcasm was."

Maddie rolled her eyes and moved over to the coffee pot. "I just love that you let yourself into my house whenever the mood strikes. What are you doing here so early in the morning?"

"What do you think?"

Maddie racked her brain, genuinely confused. "Did we have plans or something?"

"No," Christy said, shaking her head vigorously, her bright red hair brushing against her shoulders. "I'm here for the dirty details."

"What dirty details?"

Maddie was often slow on the uptake in the morning, but this morning it felt like she was wading through quicksand.

"The two-week moratorium ended yesterday," Christy said, her eyes sparkling. "I'm here to find out if more than a decade of dreaming lived up to your expectations when you and Nick finally hit the sheets."

Maddie pressed her lips together, hating the way her cheeks burned. She was feeling more comfortable with herself these days, but she was still embarrassed Christy seemed so free with the sex talk. "I think you're building this up into something it's not," she said.

"Oh, please," Christy scoffed, nonplussed. "You've been waiting for this moment forever. I want to hear every detail."

Maddie sighed and carried her mug over to the kitchen table so she could settle next to Christy. She wasn't sure how much to tell her friend. "I ... things didn't go as planned last night."

"Oh, no," Christy said, wrinkling her nose. "Was there a ... um ... technical malfunction?"

It took Maddie a moment to realize what Christy was referring to. "No! Of course not."

"Hey, Nick has been dreaming of this for just as long as you have," Christy said. "He's the one who has all the pressure on his shoulders to make sure things are perfect. If he was ... too quick ... I wouldn't worry about it. The first time is always awkward."

Maddie scowled. "We didn't get that far," she said.

"How far did you get?"

"Not far," Maddie said. "We went to dinner. It was wonderful and romantic. Then we went for a walk on the beach. Just when we were getting ready to leave ... well ... I stumbled across a dead body."

Christy, who had been nodding for each step of the story, practically spit her coffee back into the mug. "Are you kidding me?"

Maddie shook her head.

"Oh, no," Christy said, horrified. "I'm so sorry. You must be crushed. You've been waiting for this for so long. That's just ... so unfair."

"Especially for the dead girl," Maddie said.

Christy grimaced. "I ... that was really insensitive."

Maddie waved off Christy's apology. "It was horrible," she said. "The body looked like it had been in the water at some point. Trust me, even if Nick wasn't a police officer and if he didn't have to go to work, the mood would've been killed for the night."

"Did you recognize her?"

Maddie shook her head, the memory of the girl's ravaged body causing her to shudder. "No. I think they're going to have to use other means to identify her. Water can be ... brutal."

"I'm really sorry, Maddie," Christy said. "It's like you're a magnet for dead things."

Six months prior Maddie would have taken that as a personal affront. Things were different these days. Now she could recognize Christy's statement for what it really was: sympathy. "I feel bad for the woman," she said. "She looked young. I hope it was just an accident. I really do."

"Ugh." Christy made a face. "I hadn't even thought about that. Do you think she was murdered?"

Maddie merely shrugged in response. "I have no idea."

"Did you see a ghost?" Only a handful of people in Blackstone Bay were aware of Maddie's abilities, and Christy was one of them.

"No," Maddie said. "I looked around, but once the emergency personnel showed up it was really busy. I couldn't have talked to her spirit without calling attention to myself even if she was there."

"That probably means it was an accident, right?"

"Not necessarily," Maddie said. "It depends on how long the person has been dead. Ghosts have trouble controlling their new reality when they first manifest. Heck, if the woman died farther out on the lake – or in another location – her spirit might be haunting that place."

"So, unless you find out where she died, you might never know if she's a ghost," Christy mused. "Does that bother you?"

"I don't know," Maddie said. "Every time I think I don't want another ghost to approach me, I think about them wandering around without any way of crossing over and it makes me sad. Then I want them to approach me."

"It must be hard to be you," Christy said. "I keep thinking how awesome it would be to talk to ghosts, but it really does have a downside."

"It has multiple downsides," Maddie agreed. "It also feels good when it all works out."

"Speaking of feeling good, when are you and Nick going to get a chance to rub up against one another again?" Christy's eyes were twinkling. "The mood was ruined last night, but tonight is another night."

Maddie fought the urge to grin ... and lost. "I don't know," Maddie said. "Nick only got a few hours of sleep. He left an hour ago because he wanted to be there for the autopsy. Since it looks like the body was in the water, that could cause jurisdiction problems."

"I don't know what that means."

"Just because the body was found in Blackstone Bay that doesn't mean the woman died in Blackstone Bay," Maddie explained. "If she died ... or, well, was killed ... somewhere else that means multiple departments will be working together."

"Like the state police?"

Maddie nodded.

"Doesn't Nick's brother work for the state police?"

"Yeah, John," Maddie said.

"Do you know much about him?"

Maddie shrugged. "He was older than us by several years, but he was always nice to me when I was a kid," Maddie said. "Nick and John weren't very close while growing up, but I'm not sure what their relationship is like now. I never asked ... and now that you've brought it up ... I kind of feel bad about it."

"You should be publicly flogged," Christy agreed, teasing. "Tell me if he comes to town."

"John? Why? Do you know him?"

"No," Christy said. "I've seen him around, though, and let's just say those Winters genes are a thing to behold. I know Nick is the man of your dreams, but his brother is no slouch in the looks department."

Maddie rolled her eyes. "I'll ... see what I can find out."

"Good," Christy said. "Not that I don't trust you, but do you want me to make a list of the information I need you to get?"

Maddie opened her mouth to argue and then snapped it shut. "It would probably be safer."

"That's what I thought."


NICK rubbed his eyes, weary, and then turned his attention back to the file on his desk. Between the disappointment of having his date with Maddie ruined the previous evening and the lack of information on the dead girl in the file, he was having a rough morning.

"You don't look like your usual chipper self." Detective Dale Kreskin, one of the only other full-time officers on the Blackstone Bay payroll, dropped a doughnut and fresh cup of coffee on Nick's desk before settling at his own. "Trouble in paradise?"

"No," Nick said, greedily reaching for the coffee. "My paradise is intact."

Kreskin smirked. "I'm glad to see that lack of sleep isn't dampening that romantic streak you've had going since the blonde returned to town."

"The blonde has a name."

Kreskin sighed. "How is Maddie?"

"She was fine when I left her sleeping two hours ago," Nick said. "I needed to get in here and I didn't want to wake her up. She's crabby in the morning."

"Isn't everyone?"

"I guess," Nick said, rubbing the back of his neck. "Have you heard if they're done with the autopsy yet?"

"They're still in there," Kreskin said. "I heard you and Maddie were the ones who found the body. That must have put a ... crimp ... in your romantic plans."

Nick scowled. He was never one to talk about his sex life with someone else – even when there was something to brag about – but Kreskin boasted a definite lack of boundaries. "It wasn't the highlight of our night."

Pity softened Kreskin's face. "How did Maddie take it? Was she upset?"

"Of course she was upset," Nick said. "She's strong, though, and ... well ... this isn't the first dead body she's seen."

"I guess not," Kreskin said. "That whole psychic thing works against her, doesn't it?"

Nick glared at his co-worker. Blackstone Bay was full of whispers about Maddie. The residents thought she *might* be able to talk to ghosts, but they couldn't prove it. They thought she *might* be psychic, but they couldn't prove that either. They definitely thought she was odd. Nick didn't care about the gossip, but Kreskin had been relentless in recent weeks. He was determined to get Nick to admit Maddie was psychic. So far, Nick wasn't playing the game.

"Leave Maddie alone," Nick warned. "I don't want you upsetting her."

"I don't want to upset her," Kreskin said. "I just want you to admit she's psychic."

Nick glanced around, worried someone was eavesdropping. Once he was sure they were alone, he turned back to Kreskin. "I don't know what you think you know, but you're barking up the wrong tree. Leave her alone."

"Fine," Kreskin said, crossing his arms over his chest. "Tell me about the body. Did you recognize her?"

Nick shook his head. "She'd been in the water. The body was bloated and ... well ... I didn't want to get too close with Maddie there. I didn't want to give her nightmares."

"You know the state police are coming in on this, right?"

"I had a feeling," Nick said. He thought about the possibility for a moment. "If they can help us clear it faster, I'm glad they're coming."

"You just want to play kissy-face with the blonde," Kreskin said, chuckling. "Admit it."

"I have no problem admitting it," Nick said. "All I want to do these days is play kissy-face with the blonde."

"Oh, that's just what I always want to hear when I walk into a police department."

Kreskin and Nick shifted their attention to the far end of the room, their gazes falling on a new face. The state police standard blue uniform offset the man's dark coloring, and when Nick met the steady gaze of the man who looked so much like him he couldn't help but smile. "I can't believe the riffraff that the state police is sending out these days."

Kreskin frowned, worried. "I ... ."

"I can't believe the lovesick puppy keeping the fine people of Blackstone Bay safe these days," the man countered.

"I'm not a lovesick puppy."

"Who do you think you're lying to? I watched you pine for Maddie Graves for ten years. Since she came back to town I haven't gotten so much as a phone call from you." The man smiled as he moved closer to Nick's desk. "And, as your big brother, let me tell you that your lack of contact has broken our mother's heart."

Nick scowled. "You're so dramatic."

Kreskin visibly relaxed when he realized Nick and their visitor were related. "I'm Dale Kreskin."

"I'm sorry," Nick said. "That was rude. Dale, this is my brother, John."

"It's nice to meet you," John said, shaking Kreskin's hand. "I heard a lot about you before my brother ceased all contact."

"I haven't ceased all contact," Nick said. "I've been ... busy."

"I've heard," John said. "When you missed the monthly family dinner last week Mom broke the big news about you and Maddie being fused at the lips. It's ten years later than I expected it, but congratulations."

Nick rolled his eyes, but the smile on his face was goofy. "Thanks."

John turned to Kreskin. "Has my brother's head been in the clouds for the past two weeks?"

Kreskin pursed his lips, considering. "He's been happy." As much as he liked messing with Nick, he wasn't about to let anyone else do it. That was his job.

"Good," John said. "Watching him be miserable without her was starting to get old. When are you going to bring her for a family dinner? Mom is dying to see her and she doesn't want to move in too fast and crowd Maddie. She's afraid you'll freak out."

"Why would I freak out?"

"She says you're in protective mode," John replied. "I get it. You waited for her for a long time. I'm guessing you two are spending every waking minute in bed. When you come back down to Earth, you should probably try calling your mother, though. She's so desperate for information on you she's started involving herself in my personal life."

Nick snorted. "Is she trying to set you up on dates?"

"You have no idea," John said. "I've had to take three very boring women out over the past month. What she really wants is to fawn all over you and Maddie. Since she can't, she's fixating on me. I'm going to turn her loose on the two of you in exactly one week."

"Don't you dare," Nick said, wagging his finger. "We need some more time alone. Maddie isn't ready to be smothered yet."

"Isn't that what you've been doing to her?"

"Smothering her with kisses," Kreskin muttered under his breath.

John barked out a laugh. "That's what I thought."

"I'm done talking about this," Nick said. "My personal life is just that – personal. Not that I'm not glad to see you, but what are you doing here?"

"I'm here to work with you guys on the body that was found," John said, sobering. "The report that was on my desk this morning said you found it. How did that happen?"

Nick told him the story.

"That's a bummer," John said. "I'm guessing Maddie was worked up about finding a body."

"She was ... fine," Nick said, choosing his words carefully. He knew his mother was aware of Maddie's special abilities – Olivia using her close friend as a sounding board for years – but no one else in his family knew the truth. "She was upset, but it's not like she fell apart or anything."

"That's good," John said, winking at his younger brother. "Maybe tonight you can make her feel better with more of those kisses you've been smothering her with."

"Just ... let it go," Nick said. "I'm not talking to you about this."

"Oh, you're going to talk to me," John said. "You just don't know it yet. Come on. Let's go and see what the autopsy shows. Then you can fill me in on your romantic reunion with Maddie Graves. Is she as smoking hot as she was ten years ago?"

"I hate having you as a brother sometimes," Nick grumbled. "You just refuse to take no for an answer. You're so annoying."

"That's an older brother's job," John said, blasé. "You'll survive."

## 4. FOUR

"**H**ow is my girl?" Nick asked, letting himself into Magicks, the magic store Maddie ran on the main floor of her house, a little after noon and planting a light kiss on the top of his girlfriend's head.

"I'm good," Maddie said, shifting at the tarot table so she could look at Nick. The dark circles under his eyes were cause for concern. "You look tired."

"I am," Nick said. "That's part of the job, though. I'll survive."

"What are you doing here?" Maddie asked, focusing her attention on the bag he was holding. It was from a local diner, and she had a feeling she knew what was inside. "I should have brought you lunch. I wasn't thinking."

"I'm glad you didn't," Nick said. "John would have accosted you the second he saw you."

"John is here?" Maddie had to swallow the smile playing at the corner of her lips. That little tidbit was going to make Christy happy. "Is he working on the case with you?"

"He is," Nick said, sitting in the chair across from Maddie and opening the bag of food. "Until we know where she was murdered, he's going to be the lead."

Maddie's heart dropped. "She was murdered?"

"She was strangled," Nick said. "We're going to start tracking stuff down after lunch."

"Who was she?"

Nick lifted his dark eyes so he could study Maddie's face. *How much did she really want to know?* "Her name is Hayley Walker," he said. "She was sixteen."

Maddie's hands flew to her mouth, her stomach rolling painfully. "Oh, no."

"Don't get worked up, love," Nick said, reaching across the table and grabbing Maddie's hand. "It's sad, but there's nothing you could've done to stop it."

"I know," Maddie said. "I just ... she was so young."

"It wouldn't have been any better if she was in her twenties," Nick said. "Death is always sad, and murder is just ... unnecessary."

Maddie rubbed her hand against her forehead. "I know. It's just ... it always seems worse when it's someone so young. She had her whole life ahead of her. Now she's never going to know what it's like to fall in love ... or get married ... or have children. All of those dreams she had are just gone."

"I know, Mad," Nick said. "You can't focus on stuff like that."

"How do you do it? You deal with this stuff all the time."

"I don't deal with this as often as you would think," Nick said, his smile wry. "This is Blackstone Bay. In fact, until you returned to town and stumbled over a body in an alley six weeks ago, I'd never investigated a murder before."

"I wish you never had to investigate a murder."

"I wish you never had to see a dead body," Nick said. "We don't always get what we want in life. I'm just glad I got the one thing in this world I wanted more than anything else."

Maddie knew what he was getting at, but she couldn't help but give in to an inner urge and tease him. "A Ford Explorer?"

Nick snorted. "Exactly. Eat your lunch. If you hurry up, we can have exactly one hour to curl up and nap in the window seat before I have to go back to work."

"I'm not hungry," Maddie said. "I ... you should eat, though."

Nick arched an eyebrow. "I'm not hungry either, love. An hour with you is all I need to bolster me right now."

"Then move your cute butt into that window seat," Maddie said, smiling. "Afternoon naps with you are one of my favorite things in the world."

"Me, too, Mad. Me, too."

**WHEN** Nick's cell phone dinged an hour and a half later the sound was barely enough to drag him from a heavy slumber. Maddie's body was warm next to his as he spooned behind her. He groaned as he reached over and snagged the cell phone.

"What is it?" Maddie murmured.

"I have to go," Nick said, running his hand through his hair as he read the text message from his brother. "I have to notify the parents now that the identity is confirmed."

"Is that the worst part of your job?"

"I guess," Nick said, pressing his lips to Maddie's smooth jaw. "Anything that drags me away from you right now is the worst part of my job."

Maddie propped herself up on her elbow and regarded Nick with sleepy eyes. "Are you going to be working all night?"

"No," Nick replied. "I have to notify the parents and question them, but we have to wait and see what the state lab comes up with. We have no idea where this girl was or what she was doing when she died. I'll probably have to work until seven or eight, but I was thinking we could pick our date from last night up when I get done."

Maddie shifted in Nick's arms so she could face him and ran a finger down his cheek. The sleep had done him a world of good, the color returning to his cheeks and the light to his eyes, but he still looked exhausted. "Are you sure? You need sleep."

"I need you more," Nick said, kissing the tip of Maddie's nose.

"Is your brother staying in town?"

Nick narrowed his eyes at the conversational shift. "I'm not sure how I feel about you bringing up my brother when I'm trying to romance you."

A giggle erupted from Maddie's throat. "I was just wondering if he was going to be staying at your house."

Nick stilled. "Oh ... I hadn't considered that. I don't know. Crap."

"Crap what?"

"I love my brother," Nick said. "I really do. I don't want him in the next room when we ... um ... go to sleep tonight."

Maddie pursed her lips. Sleep was the last thing on Nick's mind. Actually, it was the last thing on both of their minds. The longer they waited now the bigger the build up grew. She needed him – all of him – and she had a feeling he needed her just as much. "We'll figure it out."

"How about you meet me at the station around seven and we'll decide where we're going to get dinner?" Nick suggested. "I'll know more then."

"We can always have John sleep here with Granny and you and I can go to your place."

"John was just saying how annoyed he was with having Mom set him up on blind dates," Nick said. "Maude might be exactly what he's looking for. He says he's sick of boring girls."

Maddie chortled. "Well ... if he's looking for someone fun ... I might have a suggestion."

Nick waited.

"Christy was here when I woke up this morning," Maddie said. "She expressed ... interest ... in your brother. In fact, she couldn't stop talking about the Winters genes and how impressive they are."

"Do you think the Winters genes are impressive?" Nick asked, pulling Maddie's body tighter against his.

"I'm impressed with every single thing you do," Maddie purred, pressing her lips to Nick's neck.

Nick groaned. "You know that's my sensitive spot, Mad. If you keep doing that we're going to have to go upstairs. The moratorium is over and ... well ... I'm not sure how much longer I can wait."

"You have to get back to work," Maddie reminded him.

"I'll quit."

Maddie pressed her face into the hollow between Nick's neck and shoulder briefly, inhaling deeply before kissing his sensitive spot one more time. She flicked her tongue out, enjoying the way he squirmed next to her. "I love you, Nicky."

"No one has ever loved anyone as much as I love you."

**TWENTY** minutes and a series of seriously hot kisses later Nick let himself out of the store and found Maude standing on the front porch waiting for him.

"What's going on?" Nick asked, self-consciously running his hand through his hair. Maddie's hands had a mind of their own sometimes, and that often meant his hair was a mess when she was done running her fingers through it.

"Nothing," Maude said, crossing her arms over her chest. "What makes you think something is going on?"

"You're standing on the porch staring at me."

"Oh, *that*," Maude said. "I was just waiting until you two were done groping each other in the front window of my house so I could enter without scarring any of us."

Nick's cheeks colored. "I … ."

"Oh, don't have a conniption fit," Maude said. "I'm very happy you and Maddie have managed to get over yourselves and admit that you love each other. I've been waiting for this since you two were eight and you dressed up like Prince Charming for Halloween just because she wanted to be Cinderella."

That wasn't one of Nick's favorite memories. "What's the problem then?"

"When are you going to … you know?"

If Nick thought his cheeks were burning before, they were practically on fire now. "I … we can't talk about this." Nick tried to move around Maude, but she cut off his avenue of escape.

"I don't want all the dirty details," Maude said. "I just want to know when you're going to finally make your move."

"Maude," Nick growled. "This is none of your business."

"Grow up," Maude said. "You're in love with my granddaughter and she's in love with you. It's going to happen. I just need to know if you want me to find another place to sleep tonight. I'm guessing the reason you two are still petting each other instead of really going for it is because I'm under the same roof."

Nick balked. "You're Maddie's grandmother," he said. "This is your home. What are you even getting at?"

"Well, I have an idea," Maude said, glancing at the store to make sure Maddie was busy before gesturing for Nick to follow her. It wasn't a far trip. "Open the garage door."

Nick did as instructed. When he tugged the vehicle door open he was surprised to find the mess, which had been overflowing two weeks before, was down to a more manageable pile. "I didn't know Maddie was cleaning this place out."

"She's not," Maude said. "She doesn't like the garage. She thinks it's dirty and cold. She doesn't even know I've been out here cleaning it."

"Why?"

Maude tilted her head to the side, choosing her words carefully. "Bill Schroeder came over here the other day and gave me an estimate for turning this place into an apartment. It's more than doable. I have the money. I just want to know what you think."

"You want to move to the garage?"

"I'm going to turn it into an apartment," Maude said. "I'll still use the kitchen in the house, but this would be my bedroom and we'll be putting a bathroom out here, too."

Overwhelming guilt washed over Nick. "That's not fair. I'm running you out of your own house."

"Stop that right now," Maude ordered. "I love that house. I love Maddie more. I'm well aware you two are going to move in together – and I'm guessing that's going to happen sooner rather than later."

"That doesn't mean you have to move out," Nick protested.

"I'm not moving out," Maude said. "I'm moving down a floor. And, before you start having some panic attack because you think you're forcing me out of my bedroom, that's not it."

"What is it then?"

"I'm ... getting older," Maude said, the words painful even as she said them. "It's getting harder and harder to climb those stairs every night."

"We can get one of those mechanical things that transport you up there," Nick said. "I'll buy it."

"We're never getting one of those things," Maude said, indignant. "I would rather die first."

"But ... ."

"It's going to be a great apartment," Maude said. "I won't have to climb any stairs to get into the kitchen. I'll have my own space. That means you and Maddie will have the whole top floor of the house to yourselves."

"That's not fair," Nick said. "I can't do that."

"You're not doing it," Maude said. "I am. Olivia and I were talking about doing this very thing before she died. Neither one of us wanted to move, and there's no place to put a bedroom on the main floor because of the store."

"But there are already four bedrooms."

"That's another thing," Maude said. "I want you to start talking to Maddie about moving into her mother's bedroom. She's stuck in that small closet at the far end of the hallway, and it's just not right. She should move into the master bedroom."

Nick had been trying to convince Maddie to move into her mother's room for the past two weeks. She was reticent, so he'd given up trying ... for now. "Are you sure you want to do this, Maude?"

"I'm sure," Maude said. "We're still a family. You two don't need me on top of you, though, and I don't want Maddie on top of me when I have overnight guests of the male persuasion."

Nick shuddered at the visual. "I ... ."

"It's still going to take about a month for the construction to be completed," Maude said. "I'm going to tell Maddie today. I just want to be able to tell her you're on board with my decision when I do."

"I'm on board with anything you want," Nick said. "I love you. I just can't help feeling like I'm forcing you out of your own house."

"Oh, you're cute," Maude said. "We both know you couldn't force me into anything I didn't want."

She was right on that front. "Thank you, Maude," Nick said, sincere.

"No," Maude said. "Thank you. Maddie has never been this happy. You just need to keep it up. If I never see that girl sad again it will be too soon."

That was something they could both agree on.

## 5. FIVE

"What are you doing here?" Christy asked, lifting a quizzical eyebrow as Maddie walked through the front door of Cuts & Curls. "Is something wrong?"

"I was hoping you could trim my hair so it looks good for tonight."

Christy twirled in her salon chair and focused on Maddie, a sly smile spreading across her face. "Is tonight *the* night?"

"Maybe," Maddie said, averting her eyes from Christy's probing gaze. "I ... if you're busy ... ."

Christy gestured at the empty salon. "Do I look busy?"

"Where is everyone?"

"It's just one of those weird lulls," Christy said. "I told you I prefer to schedule most of my appointments before lunch so I can leave early. It happened today."

"Why are you still here?"

"I realized I have nothing to do at home."

Maddie grinned. "Well, if you trim my hair, I might have some other gossip to share with you."

Christy brightened considerably and jumped out of the chair. "Sit your cute little bottom down and spill."

Once Maddie was settled Christy draped the protective smock

over her and turned her so they could face each other in the mirror. "What's the big gossip?"

Maddie had two tidbits to share, and she wasn't sure which one should get top billing. "Granny sat me down for a talk today."

"Oh, the birds and the bees?"

Maddie smirked. "No. She's decided to turn the garage into an apartment and move into it."

Christy stilled, surprised. "Really? Why?"

"Well, at first I thought it was because she felt uncomfortable with Nick spending the night all the time."

"That doesn't sound like her at all," Christy said. "She's got today in the pool for when you guys finally do it, and I know she's chomping at the bit to make sure she wins this one. She's still mad I won the last one."

Maddie frowned. "You guys have another pool?" Two weeks before Maddie found out that everyone in town was betting on when she and Nick would hook up. Christy ultimately won – and proceeded to buy three pairs of expensive shoes. Knowing another pool was ongoing was grating, to say the least.

"It's Blackstone Bay, Maddie," Christy said. "There are pools for everything. It's not just about you and Nick."

"Really? What other pools are ongoing?"

"There's a pool for when Maude and Harriet Proctor are going to throw down next. There's a pool for when Edgar Wadsworth is going to realize that none of his zippers stay up. There's a pool for when Penny Nelson gives in and starts wearing a bra."

Maddie made a face. "Are you serious? How come I don't know about any of these pools?"

"People think you're too sweet," Christy said. "They're afraid you'll look down on them if they approach you."

Maddie wasn't sure if that was a compliment or a dig so she let it slide. "Do you want to hear the rest of my story?"

"Continue," Christy said, her eyes flashing with delight. Maddie really was starting to find her footing in life.

"Granny said she's been having trouble climbing the steps for some time," Maddie said. "I actually feel guilty about that because I had no idea she was struggling. I would have put one of those mechanical lifts in for her."

"Those things are ugly."

"I don't care," Maddie said. "My grandmother was in pain every time she had to climb those steps."

Christy's face softened. "I know. That's horrible. I should have realized it, too. I just never thought about it."

"I guess she and Mom were talking about converting the garage when Mom died," Maddie said. "She's already gotten an estimate on it. It's going to be done in about five weeks. This way she'll still have access to the main floor of the house, but she won't have to climb any steps."

"Or hear you and Nick rattling headboards."

"Don't go to a gross place right now," Maddie said. "We're talking about my grandmother's health."

"Maude wants you to start rattling headboards," Christy countered. "It will make her feel better when you finally do."

Maddie rolled her eyes. "I almost think I shouldn't tell you the other piece of gossip I picked up this afternoon because you're being so mean to me."

"I'm sorry," Christy said, instantly contrite. "You're right. I'm crass and horrible. I'm a terrible friend."

"You're a great friend," Maddie argued. "You're just really obnoxious sometimes."

"That's what makes me a great friend."

"Do you want to know or not?"

"Fine," Christy said with an exaggerated sigh. "What other gossip do you have?"

"The body we found last night belonged to a local teenager," Maddie said. "Her name was Hayley Walker."

"Oh, no," Christy said, sobering. "That's awful."

"Did you know her?"

"She was a nice girl," Christy said. "Quiet. I think she was a member of the band."

"She was strangled."

"Oh ... God ... ." Christy's eyes darkened. "What kind of animal would do something like that?"

"I have no idea," Maddie said. "Nick was going to talk to her family after lunch."

"Well, keep me updated," Christy said. "I'm going to want to send her mother some flowers. She's a regular client."

"That wasn't actually my gossip," Maddie said. "It was just the lead up to my gossip."

"You're getting much better at being a normal woman," Christy said. "You're learning about dramatic delivery and everything."

Maddie narrowed her eyes. "Do you want to know the rest of the gossip?"

"I guess," Christy said, feigning indifference. "I don't know how you're going to top the first two things."

"The state police sent an officer to work on the case," Maddie said, enjoying the way Christy's body stiffened in anticipation. "It's John Winters. He's going to be in town until the case is solved."

Christy's smile was sly. "I'm finally going to get my chance with a Winters man," she said. "It's finally happening. Hallelujah!" Christy shook her fist at the ceiling.

"You're unbelievable."

The sound of the bell jangling over the door caused both women to shift their attention to the front of the parlor. The two women standing there were enough to make Maddie's heart plummet. Marla Proctor and Cassidy Dunham, aka the one person who always knew just how to upset Maddie and the one person who Maddie had managed to emotionally crush.

"Well, well, well," Marla said, hands on hips. "What's going on here?"

Christy snipped the scissors in her hand twice for emphasis. "It's called a haircut."

"I can't believe you have the audacity to show your face here," Marla said, ignoring Christy's snark. "After what you did to poor Cassidy here, you should be hiding under a rock."

Maddie bit the inside of her cheek, conflicted.

"Marla, you and I have had this conversation before," Christy warned. "If you can't be polite to my customers – especially Maddie – then you can find another place to get your hair done. I'm not joking."

That was a significant threat because Cuts & Curls was the only salon within an hour's driving distance in any direction. It was one of the most popular places in town, and Christy enjoyed holding court with her gaggle of gossips every morning. She was revered as a queen in these parts – and that's the way she liked it.

"Don't you threaten me," Marla said. She was clearly feeling superior today. Since her last boyfriend – who she was touting as a financial dynamo – had been arrested for money laundering and hauled away, her attitude had gone from bad to worse.

"I can do whatever I want in my business," Christy said. "Do you see that sign on the door? It says I have the right to refuse service to anyone. That includes you."

"Whatever," Marla said. "I would think you'd be worried about your business collapsing because you continue to associate with this ... homewrecker."

Maddie pressed her eyes shut, mortified. Nick's dumping of Cassidy had been epic – and the stuff town gossip was made for. Once realizing Nick was going to break up with her Cassidy had a mini meltdown and hid from him for days. Then, when the time finally came, she broke into his house, wearing nothing but lingerie, and threw herself at him in the hopes he would somehow change his mind. When that didn't happen, she had another meltdown. Maddie hadn't seen her in almost two weeks. With Marla whispering sweet nastiness into her ear, Maddie was certain things were about to spiral out of control. Again.

"Get out," Christy said, furious.

"Excuse me?" Marla wasn't backing down. "Are you saying Maddie isn't a homewrecker?"

"That's exactly what I'm saying," Christy said. "Cassidy, I'm truly sorry you got hurt and were so ... embarrassed ... but you did a lot of it to yourself. You and Nick weren't married, though, and he was going to break up with you before Maddie even returned to town.

"Blaming Maddie for something that was going to happen whether she came back or not isn't fair," Christy continued. "It's also a little ... deranged. You just need to get over it."

Cassidy finally spoke. "Get over it? How am I supposed to get over this *woman* coming into town and stealing what was mine?"

"He was never yours," Christy replied, nonplussed. "He was always Maddie's. Everyone in this town knows it. Nick knows it. Marla knows it. If she's telling you something else ... well ... then she's doing it for her own personal reasons."

"That's completely untrue," Marla said, incensed. "Maddie knows what she did. I have no idea how she can live with herself."

"How do you live with yourself?" Christy shot back. "Do you want to know what I think is going on?"

"Not particularly."

"I think you're still holding a grudge because you had the hots for Nick in high school and he ignored you," Christy said, not missing a beat. "You panted after him. You tried to rub yourself against him. He never had eyes for anyone but Maddie, though. That made you bitter."

"You take that back," Marla said. "That's not ... that's ... Maddie is the one in the wrong here."

"Maddie isn't in the wrong," Christy said. "I'm not even sure Cassidy is in the wrong. Sure, she acted a little ... immaturely ... when this all shook out. We all do things we're ashamed of, though. You're the one in the wrong, Marla. You always have been where Maddie is concerned. It's pathetic."

Maddie risked a look in Cassidy's direction. "I'm sorry you were hurt," she said, her voice small. "I'm not sorry for being with Nick, though. We're happy. I don't want to make you feel bad, but I'm not going to apologize for being happy."

Christy was impressed. It wasn't the verbal smackdown she wanted Maddie to put on Marla, but it also wasn't the cowering she'd become accustomed to when Maddie was confronted with unrest.

"I suppose Nick is happy, too," Cassidy said, making a face. "He finally has what he always wanted. Of course, he's happy. What am I even saying?"

"I think I should be going," Maddie said, reaching for the back of the smock. "My hair is fine."

"Are you sure?" Christy asked. "I'll wrestle Marla out of here if you give me five minutes."

"I'm sure," Maddie said. "I don't want to deal with this. I'm just ... done ... dealing with this. Nothing good is going to come out of another fight." Maddie hopped out of the chair and moved toward the door. "I'll call you tomorrow."

"I want all the details," Christy said, forcing a smile.

"I'll do my best," Maddie said, giving Cassidy and Marla a wide berth as she circled around them. "I really am sorry for everything I did to you, Cassidy. When you asked me about my feelings where Nick was concerned I shouldn't have lied. If it's any consolation, I didn't mean for you to get caught up in all of our ... drama."

"It's not any consolation," Cassidy said, her lower lip trembling. "I'm still the one who lost the man she loved."

"I'm sorry," Maddie repeated. "I hope that you find some peace ... and I hope you find it soon."

"And I hope you find the karma that's coming to you," Marla snapped.

Maddie ignored her as she exited the parlor. Once she was gone, Christy fixed Marla with a dark look. "When are you going to grow up?"

"I have no idea what you're talking about," Marla sniffed. "I need you to set my hair, though. We're going out to the bar tonight and I need to look good."

"You'd better start driving now then," Christy said. "You're going to have to find another beauty parlor, and I think the closest one is over in Suttons Bay. Have fun with your drive."

"You can't be serious," Marla said, tapping her foot on the floor. "I need my hair done now."

"Oh, I'm serious," Christy said. "I want you out of here now ... and don't ever come back."

"What? You're banning me again?"

"It's a lifetime ban," Christy said. "You're not welcome here." She glanced at Cassidy, pity washing over her. "When you come back to your senses you can return. As long as you're going to keep attacking Maddie I can't allow it, though. You need to stop listening to whatever nonsense Marla is spouting and think for yourself. I think, when you do, you'll realize that Maddie never took anything from you. She just gave in and embraced what was already hers."

"I can't believe you're doing this," Marla screeched.

"Believe it," Christy said. "Now get out."

## 6. SIX

"That's one conversation I never want to have again," Nick said, keeping his head low as he moved toward his Ford Explorer.

"It's never easy telling parents they've lost their child," John agreed, opening the passenger side door and hopping in. "Those two seemed ... stoic. It could've been worse."

"I think they might've been in shock."

"I think you're probably right," John said. "I'm sure there are some emotional breakdowns in their future, and the way the father headed straight for the whiskey was a tipoff that he's going to deal with it by drinking his dinner tonight."

Once both vehicle doors were shut, Nick turned to John with a serious expression on his face. "Are you bothered by the fact that the kid was missing for two weeks and the parents didn't say anything about it?"

"I can't decide," John said. "From the sounds of it, the kid was kind of wild. The mother said she had a lot of boyfriends and she was known for doing whatever the hell she wanted whenever the hell she wanted to do it."

"She was still only sixteen," Nick pointed out.

"The parents say they thought she was staying with a friend."

"Do you believe them?"

"Until we know more, I don't see where we have a lot of choice in the matter," John said. "I mean, she's been missing for two weeks, but the coroner thinks she was killed before midnight yesterday. That's a long time for them to have locked her away." He glanced at the Explorer's console. "How about we run down to the marina and ask a few questions and then get a bite to eat there? We can get a drink once we're done. I've got plain clothes to change into in the back."

Nick faltered. "I ... kind of made plans with Maddie."

John rolled his eyes. "Don't you make plans with Maddie every night?"

"Yes ... but ... ."

"No buts," John said. "You and I are going out together tonight. If you want to invite Maddie, go nuts. I'd kind of like to see her."

"I ... ."

"You can go one night without rolling around naked with your beloved blonde," John said. "You're going to have a whole lifetime to do that."

"How do you know that?"

"Because I've always known you two would end up together," John said. "Everyone knew that. One night away from her isn't going to kill you."

Nick wasn't so sure, but there was no way he could tell his brother the real reason he was so desperate to spend the night with Maddie. "I'll call her," he said, resigned. "If she's upset, though, you're on your own."

"Oh, suck it," John said. "She's an adult. I'm sure she can find a way to entertain herself for one night. I'm your brother. We need some bonding time."

"Bonding time?"

"I'm just dying to hear how all of this happened," John admitted. "I'm not sure Mom has all the gory details correct."

"You might be surprised," Nick said. "She seems up on all the town gossip. She even put money in the pool to see when we would get together."

John snorted. "I lost. I was way off. I thought you guys would fight it for at least another two months. I forgot to take your desperation into consideration."

Nick shot his brother a look. "You were in the pool?"

"We all have to entertain ourselves the best way we can," John said. "Now ... drive. Now that I've mentioned eating down by the marina all I can think about is crab legs."

Unfortunately for Nick, all he could think about was something that he probably wasn't going to get ... at least not tonight.

**BLACKSTONE BAY** is one of those small towns that has just about everything to offer – except progress. The storefronts are quaint, the side streets made out of cobblestone, and the water is expansive.

In addition to the huge lake, the hamlet also offered various rivers, ponds and other smaller lakes to entice the local population. The town was a coveted destination in the summer and a quiet place to snowmobile, ski, and ice skate in the winter.

It was a beautiful area, and one of the best spots to visit was Blackstone Marina. Most local denizens owned boats – even if they were small fishing boats – but a handful of the more affluent denizens rented slips at the marina for the summer months.

"I haven't been here in almost two years," John admitted, striding down the impressive fishing pier and scanning the regulars with a smile. "I used to love coming here when we were kids."

"It's nice," Nick said, noncommittal. "I prefer the lake behind Maddie's house, though. It's more private."

John arched an eyebrow. "What have you two been doing in the lake?"

Nick smiled. While sex had been off the menu, skinny-dipping had not. Nick had seen everything he was missing – on multiple occasions – and he was still annoyed it looked like he would be missing it again. He'd called Maddie, but she hadn't picked up, so he'd been forced to leave a bittersweet message. He was hoping against hope she would go against her better nature and not understand. If she pitched a fit he'd have a reason to abandon his brother for the evening.

"That's an absolutely adorable smile," John said, studying his brother. "I'm guessing the lake has been serving as your personal playground – especially with it being so hot lately."

Nick forced himself to return to the present. "We loved that lake long before we started dating."

"I remember," John said. "I kept sneaking down there in the hopes I would catch you two doing something. Even when I came back for summers when I was in college I was sure I would finally find you two ... doing something. Usually, I just found you catching turtles and talking. You two were the most boring teenagers ever."

"Thanks."

"Poor, baby brother," John said, reaching over and snagging Nick's cheek. "You're just so under appreciated."

Nick jerked his cheek away. "I'll have you know, we weren't boring teenagers," he said. "We had a great time together."

"I know you did," John said. "You were still geeks."

"Don't ever say anything bad about my Maddie," Nick warned. "I don't like it, and I'm going to have to beat you to a bloody pulp if you continue to do it."

"You're so happy it's sickening," John said, smiling. "I'm happy for you."

"Thank you," Nick said, averting his gaze. "I'm happy for me, too."

"So, when are you going to propose?"

Nick shook his head, dumbfounded. "Seriously? We've been together for two weeks."

"You've been in love with her for your entire life."

Nick shrugged. "I'd propose right now," he said. "She's all I want. I don't want to rush it, though. I want to be able to enjoy dating her. I want to enjoy moving in together. There's no reason to hurry."

"Are you afraid she's going to run again?"

It was a serious question, and Nick had silently asked it more than once. The truth was, though, he wasn't scared of that. He knew why Maddie ran the first time, and however misguided, she'd never wanted to leave him. "No. She's home. We're home."

"Okay, if you're not going to propose right away, when are you two going to move in together?"

"Soon," Nick said, thinking back on his conversation with Maude. "That brings up an interesting topic, though."

"Can I have your house?"

Nick grinned. His house was on the Blackstone River, and everyone in the family had been crestfallen when his grandfather left it to him after passing. It was a coveted house, and even though Nick loved it he knew his future with Maddie wouldn't be spent there. "I'll sell it to you."

John was taken aback. "You will? Aren't you two going to move out there? I was just joking when I asked for it."

"No," Nick said. "Maddie's business is in her house. Maude is in that house, although she's building a separate apartment in the garage. The lake is right behind Maddie's house, and the woods that she loves are right there. We'll be living there."

"You've already thought this out," John said, impressed.

"When you've been dreaming about something as long as I have, you figure things out quickly," Nick said. "When I picture my future with Maddie it's in her house. I'd like to keep my house in our family, so if you're interested in buying it, I'm sure there's something we can work out."

"I love that house," John said. "I definitely want to buy it. It might take me a few months to unload my house, though."

"That's fine," Nick said. "Maude's apartment isn't going to be ready for another five or six weeks."

"Are you going to ask her or are you just going to move all of your stuff in when she's not looking?" John teased.

"We have to have a talk about it," Nick said, serious. "She's still sleeping in her bedroom."

"And that's a problem?"

"It's tiny," Nick explained. "There's not enough room for her stuff in there, let alone mine."

"Ah," John said, realization dawning. "You want her to move into Olivia's old bedroom."

"I'd like to upgrade the bathroom first," Nick said. "I'd also like to have the hardwood floors buffed and the room painted, but I'd at least like a firm commitment from Maddie where that room is concerned."

"Have you talked about it?"

"Not about us moving into it," Nick said. "I have brought up her moving a few times."

"And?"

"She feels like she's ... displacing ... her mother."

"Olivia is dead, though."

Nick couldn't tell his brother that even though Olivia was dead, that didn't mean she still wasn't hanging around. He would never understand. "I know," Nick said. "It hasn't been that long. I'm going to talk to her."

"Maddie wants to make you happy just as much as you want to make her happy," John said. "You're adults now. I think you're going to find planning a life together to be a lot easier than you think it's going to be."

"I don't care how easy it is," Nick said. "I want it. We'll make it work." He tilted his chin toward the far end of the pier. "Let's go talk to them. They're regulars. If anyone saw something I'm going to bet it's them."

"Let's go, Romeo," John said, smiling. "See if you can charm them as easily as you charmed Miss Maddie."

**"YOU KNOW** who you want to talk to? Raymond Jacob Kingston."

Mildred Donahue was a regular fixture on the Blackstone pier. In addition to being one of Maude's Pink Ladies, she was also the one woman in town who could keep up with the local Knights of Columbus chapter when they decided to tap a keg. Unlike Maude, though, she liked to spend her afternoons fishing instead of stirring up trouble.

"Who is that?" John asked.

"He's a local fisherman," Nick replied. "He moved here about three years ago. He lives out on Cunningham Road."

"He's a pervert," Mildred said. "If something bad happened to a young girl, he's the one who did it. Mark my words."

Nick frowned. "Define ... pervert."

"He has sexual inclinations that make me sick to my stomach," Mildred replied. "He also has roaming fingers."

"I understand what a pervert is," Nick said, choosing his words carefully. "I want to know why you think Ray is one."

"Whenever the young girls are on the pier he hits on them," Mildred said. "He says stuff about wanting to bait their hooks. He's also friendly with the butt pats."

Nick made a face.

"How old is this Raymond Jacob Kingston?" John asked.

"He's in his seventies," Nick said. "He's too old to be patting the butts of teenage girls."

"Oh, he doesn't pat *their* butts," Mildred said. "Don't get me wrong, if he was quick enough to catch one of them he would probably try. They always manage to evade him, though. He's built up quite the reputation down here."

"I don't understand," Nick said. "Whose butt is he patting?"

"He's always trying to pat my butt and ... trust me ... no one wants that. It's not even as high up as it used to be."

John pursed his lips to keep from laughing out loud. "Where can we find Raymond?"

Mildred tilted her head to the side, considering. "It's interesting that you ask," she said. "I haven't seen him in a few days now."

"How many days?" Nick asked, interested.

"It's been at least two," Mildred said. "The only reason I even noticed is because he's always here."

John and Nick exchanged a look.

"Do me a favor, Mildred," Nick said, pulling a business card out of his back pocket. "If you see Raymond, don't say anything to him. Just call me."

"You've got it," Mildred said, pocketing the card. "I am sad to hear about that girl. I didn't know her other than recognizing her from afar, but that's a horrible way to die."

"It is," Nick agreed.

"Oh, before you go, I'm just desperate to know when you plan on finally going all the way with the Graves girl," Mildred said. "I've got Sunday in the pool, so if you can hold off until then, that would be great. I've got my eye on a custom fishing pole, and the money will just about cover it."

Nick's neck burned under John's studied gaze. "I'll keep that in mind," he said stiffly. "Have a nice day."

"I see we have a few more things to talk about," John said. "You've been holding out on me."

Nick desperately wished a hole would open up underneath him and swallow him whole. He so didn't want to have this conversation.

## 7. SEVEN

"So, do you want to tell me why you've spent two weeks sharing a bed with the love of your life and you haven't made a move yet?" John leaned back in his chair and fixed his younger with a serious look.

Nick had been dreading this conversation for more than an hour. After changing his clothes, John picked a local restaurant so they could eat and have a few drinks. Dinner conversation had been light, most of it revolving around the case, and Nick had almost managed to convince himself that John was going to let Mildred's parting shot go unnoticed.

He wasn't that lucky.

"I'm not talking about this," Nick said.

"You're talking about it," John said. "When I thought the reason you missed family dinner was because you were spending the entire day in bed with Maddie I understood your actions. I don't understand ... this."

"What's to understand?" Nick asked, leaning back in his chair and sipping from his beer. "We're taking our time."

"Why really?"

Nick sighed, pinching the bridge of his nose to ward off the headache he was sure was coming. "Because she was ... nervous ... when I admitted I loved her," he said. "She was scared."

John furrowed his brow. "What was she scared of?"

"She thought I was going to get bored with her," Nick said. "And if I got bored with her ... ."

"Then you could never go back to what you had," John finished. "I get it. Still ... I would've thought you two would just do it that first night. You've had ten years of ... need ... building up."

"I wanted her to get comfortable with me first."

"I've never seen her anything but comfortable with you."

"This was different," Nick said. "I didn't want her constantly thinking about that when she could be focusing on just ... feeling. That's why I put a moratorium on sex."

John pursed his lips, amused. "For how long?"

"Two weeks," Nick said. "I wanted time for us just to be a couple without anything hanging over us."

"And?"

"And it was the best two weeks of my life."

"When is the moratorium over?"

"Last night," Nick said.

John barked out a hoarse laugh. "So, let me get this straight," he said. "You've pined after Maddie Graves for a decade. You finally got her, but you put a moratorium on sex because you wanted her to be comfortable. The moratorium was finally over, and then she stumbled across a dead body. Am I getting this right?"

"Pretty much."

John guffawed loudly. "You poor man."

"Let it go," Nick said. "I'm not going to sit here and let you make fun of me. I don't care what you say. I have everything I've ever wanted."

"You're still missing one thing," John pointed out.

"No, I'm not," Nick said. "The only thing I need every night is her next to me."

"You're so sappy."

"No, I'm happy," Nick said. "I don't care what anyone else thinks. I just care what Maddie thinks."

"That's probably why she's been in love with you since she was sixteen," John said. "And, yes, I noticed she was in love with you before I realized you loved her back. It took you longer than it took her."

"It didn't take me longer," Nick corrected. "I've always loved her. I just didn't realize the difference between loving someone and being in love with them."

"That's a good answer," John said. "Why didn't you tell her before she left for college?"

"Because she wasn't ready to hear it," Nick said. "She was ... dealing with some stuff. I know how I acted when she left. I'm not ashamed to say she broke my heart because she did."

"I know that," John said. "Trust me. I saw you ... crumble. Was it hard for you to forgive her?"

"I forgave her the second I saw her," Nick said. "It took me a week to realize that I'd already forgiven her, but ... it was like no time had passed. I saw her face and ... I was just done. I fought my feelings because I didn't want to forgive her. I thought it made me weak."

"And now?"

"And now I know that she's the one thing in this world that truly gives me strength."

"You're suddenly a poet," John teased. "Still, it must drive you crazy knowing that the two of you wasted ten years."

"I'm not sure we did," Nick said. "Mom and I had a talk a few weeks ago. She knew why Maddie left all along. Olivia told her."

"Why did Maddie leave?"

"I'm not telling you that," Nick said. "It's her secret."

"Good enough," John said. "What did Mom say to you?"

"She said that Maddie and I wouldn't have survived as a couple then because we were too young," Nick said. "She said we weren't ready for life together, and by being separated then we made sure we were mature enough to love one another as adults now."

"Do you think that's true?"

"I was mad at first," Nick admitted. "I thought she ... robbed ... me of something. She was right, though. I wouldn't trade my life now for anything in this world."

John grinned. "You're so happy I want to puke."

"Join the club."

Nick jolted at the sound of the new voice, lifting his eyes to Christy's expressive face and gracing her with a small smile. "What are you doing here? Is Maddie with you?"

"I thought Maddie was with you," Christy said, grabbing the open chair between John and Nick and settling in it. "Why are you here, by the way?"

"My brother wanted dinner and a drink."

"Ah," Christy said, nodding and turning in John's direction. "You're the elusive John Winters. I've been dying to meet you."

Nick smirked. Christy was known as something of a flirt, and the look she was giving John now was nothing short of scandalous. "Do you want a drink?"

"Sure," Christy said, not moving her eyes from John. "I'll have whatever you guys are having. I'm ... easy."

"That's the word on the street," Nick teased, rolling his eyes. "John, if you don't remember her, this is Christy Ford. She graduated with Maddie and me."

"I think I kind of remember you," John said, smiling. "I definitely remember that red hair."

Nick was starting to feel like a fifth wheel. Since John appeared to be charmed by Christy, Nick saw an out for himself, though. Another beer and these two would be well on their way to a comfortable evening of flirting. That would allow him the chance to sneak out and find Maddie. That's all he could think about right now.

**AN HOUR** later Nick was starting to lay the groundwork for his escape. The problem was, Christy and John were so busy with their own conversation they wouldn't let him get a word in edgewise. He was considering just leaving and then sending John a text once he was safely on the road. He was pretty sure Christy would make sure he had a ride home.

"Well, well, well. Look who it is."

Nick internally cringed when he heard Marla's voice, refusing to turn around and give her the satisfaction of acknowledging her presence.

John lifted a friendly eyebrow. "Um ... do I know you?"

"No," Marla said. "I definitely want to know you, though."

"I'm sure you do," Christy said. "We're full up here, though."

"Oh, Christy, don't be that way," Marla said. "I'm sure you can find room for Cassidy and I to sit down."

Since he'd been staring at the table Nick didn't realize Marla wasn't alone. Now he was really wishing he'd snuck out when he had the chance.

"Hello, Nick," Cassidy said, her voice low. "How are you?"

"I'm fine," Nick said. "How are you?"

John watched Nick interact with the women, confused. He leaned over so he could whisper to Christy. "What's going on?"

"You don't know who that is?" Christy asked.

John shook his head.

"Oh, well, this will be fun," Christy said. "Okay, where to start? The tall bitchy one is Marla Proctor. She spent her teenage years panting after Nick and hating on Maddie. She was really mean to her. I mean ... like ... horrible."

John nodded, soaking it all in. "Go on."

"The other girl is Cassidy Dunham," Christy said. "She's the girl Nick was dating when Maddie came back to town."

"Oh, she's the girl who had the meltdown when Nick dumped her," John said. "Mom told me about her. I think she broke into his house."

"She did," Christy said. "She's also had some *choice* words for Maddie."

"Do you blame her?"

"I don't know," Christy said. "People warned her when she started dating Nick that it wouldn't end well. Everyone – and I mean everyone – in town knew he had a six-month cycle. What I don't get is why you never met her."

"I've never met any of them," John said. "Part of his cycle was to make sure the girls never interacted with our family. He didn't want them to have unrealistic expectations – like they would ever see us again."

Christy snickered. "I guess that makes sense."

"Have Nick and Cassidy seen each other since the breakup?"

"I think there was an uncomfortable run-in two nights after the mortifying lingerie incident," Christy said. "Since then? I don't think so."

"Oh, fun," John said. "Nick looks like he wants to crawl into a hole and die. Why is Cassidy friends with this Marla girl if she's so horrible?"

"I think Cassidy just wants to hang around with someone who hates Maddie as much as she does," Christy replied. "Marla fits the bill. What Cassidy doesn't realize is that Marla would've snaked Nick from her in a second if she got the chance."

"Interesting," John said. "You are an endless source of information."

"I like to gossip."

John smiled. "You're cute, too."

Christy smiled right back at him. "You have excellent eyesight."

Nick watched Christy and John chat out of the corner of his eye, silently cursing them both. Didn't they see he was floundering here?

"How are ... things ... in your life, Cassidy?"

"Oh, they're great," Cassidy said. "Everyone in the town walks around laughing at me and I try to keep my head down so they don't recognize me. It's constant work."

Nick scowled. "I'm sorry to hear that."

"So, where is your homewrecker girlfriend?" Marla asked, changing the subject. "I thought she was in Christy's salon getting her hair done because she had a big date with you tonight. That's the way she made it sound."

Nick shot John a challenging look. "I thought we had a date, too."

John ignored him.

"Oh, this is just priceless," Marla said, clapping her hands. "Maddie spent her afternoon getting ready for a date and you're already bored with her. It couldn't have happened to a nicer homewrecker."

"I'm not bored with her," Nick said. "My brother is in town. He wanted to go out. I had no choice in the matter."

"That's true," John said, trying to be helpful. "I made him abandon the blonde for the night."

"I'll bet she's home crying," Marla said. "She doesn't know what to do with herself when Nick and Christy aren't around. I can't wait until it gets back to her that we were all out together."

Nick froze, the gravity of Marla's words washing over him. "That's not going to happen," he said, pushing his chair back and getting to his feet. "I'm officially done here."

"Now ... wait," John said, desperate for his time with Christy to continue. "What about me? I need a ride back to your place."

"You're not staying with me," Nick said matter-of-factly. "You're going to a hotel."

"No way," John said. "The only hotel the state will pay for is that dive out on the highway."

"Then stay with Christy," Nick said, guileless. "She's got a nice house ... and I'm sure she'd love the company."

Christy shot Nick an appreciative look. "I'll make sure he finds a place to land tonight."

"I'm sure you will."

"I have room at my house," Marla offered.

"He had crabs when he was in high school," Nick said. "I don't think he wants them again."

Christy snorted into her drink while John made a face. "Thanks for telling people *that* story."

"Whatever," Nick said. "I'm going to get my girl."

"You should," Christy said. "After running into these two this afternoon she's probably feeling a little sad."

Now Nick felt doubly guilty. No wonder she hadn't returned his call. He fixed John with a serious look. "Do not come out to my house. I don't care if your pants are on fire – which they will be if you touch Marla, by the way. Don't come out to that house. It's not yours yet."

John's eyes were soft as he regarded his younger brother. "Have the night of your life, man."

"Have the night of both of your lives," Christy said, beaming.

"Wait a second," Marla said, hands on hips. "What about us?"

"I'm sure there are some guys down on the pier who will give you the night of your life, Marla," Christy said. "Some of them might even have teeth."

Nick was practically giddy as he left his brother in Christy's capable hands. Tonight was the night. He was ready for the next step.

## 8. EIGHT

"Nick?"

Maddie was in her pajamas, her blonde hair pulled away from her makeup-free face and ready for bed when Nick texted her. The message was brief: *Come to my house.*

Worried, Maddie didn't bother changing out of her pajamas before jumping in her car and racing out to Nick's secluded house. She was worried. *Had he hurt himself? Was he upset? Was something else wrong?*

Maddie's heart pounded painfully hard when she let herself in through the front door with the key Nick bestowed upon her weeks before. The living room was empty. As much time as they'd shared together over the past two weeks, Maddie had only spent the night out here twice, so she wasn't familiar with the way he kept things. She felt weird wandering around Nick's house without him – like she was invading his personal space.

"Nick?"

There was no answer. She hurried to his bedroom, frowning when she found it empty. *Where is he?*

"Nick?"

She was about to leave and search the rest of the house when the glint of something on the back lawn caught her attention. Nick's house wasn't big – only two bedrooms – and the expansive back deck was accessible through a set of sliding glass doors in his bedroom.

Maddie moved closer to the glass door and peered out. What she saw was enough to steal the air from her lungs.

Nick was sitting on the lush grass, a blanket spread out beneath him. There were candles – at least twenty of them – and they were flickering in the night sky and beckoning to her.

Maddie took a deep breath and slid the door open, stepping out onto the deck and staring at Nick's strong back for a moment. She knew what this was, and other than her outfit, she'd never been more ready for anything in her entire life.

**NICK** shifted his head so he could stare at the house when he heard the door slide open. There she was ... his Maddie. She was dressed in fuzzy pajama pants, a tank top, and a simple black hoodie. Her hair was pulled away from her face, which was just how he liked it: devoid of makeup. She was dressed down, and yet he'd never seen anything more beautiful.

"You scared me," Maddie said, walking down the lawn until she reached the blanket. She put her hands on her hips as she stared down at him. "I thought something happened to you."

"Something did happen to me," Nick said, patting the blanket next to him. "I fell in love with you."

Maddie sighed. "I'm trying to pretend like I'm angry with you. You're making it hard."

"That's the plan," Nick said, smirking. "Come on, love. Sit with me."

Maddie gladly joined him on the blanket, smiling as he wrapped his arm around her waist and drew her close. "I thought you were spending the evening with your brother. That's what your message said."

"Yeah, well, that's not what I wanted to be doing," Nick said, brushing his lips against her ear and causing her to shudder. "John insisted. I was actually hoping you would put up a fight and demand my attention this evening."

"That seemed juvenile."

"I know," Nick said, rubbing his thumb against her soft cheek. "Christy showed up at the restaurant and saved me, though. I'm going to have to buy her another bouquet of flowers as a thank you."

Maddie arched an eyebrow. "She did?"

"It seems she might have a thing for my brother."

"I knew that," Maddie said, her eyes sparkling. "She wanted me to introduce her to him. I told you that this afternoon."

"She introduced herself," Nick said. "Trust me. She made an impression. He's either staying at a hotel or her house tonight."

"But ... they just met."

Nick grinned. "Not everyone wants to wait, Mad."

"Are you sad we waited?"

"I'm not sad about anything," Nick said. "Are you sad we waited?"

"I've never been happier in my entire life," Maddie replied. "I just wish you'd told me what you had planned. I wouldn't have worn ... this."

Nick pulled her tighter against him. "I don't care about that, Mad. You're always going to be the prettiest woman in the world. Besides, I don't plan on letting you wear it long."

"Are we ... doing it here?"

"No," Nick said, kissing her cheek again. "I just want a few minutes with you before we go inside. I like the sound of the water. It relaxes me."

"I'm surprised you don't want to do it here," Maddie said, her eyes wide. "It's beautiful. You lit candles. I didn't know you were shy about doing it outside."

"I'm not shy about doing it outside," Nick said. "I'm sure we will do it outside. I've had fantasies about the lake for as long as I can remember, and we still have some nice summer weeks in front of us."

"But?"

"But this is our first time," Nick said. "I want our first time to be ... perfect."

. . .

**MADDIE'S** heart swelled at Nick's words, and her voice caught in her throat because she was so overcome with emotion. "There's no such thing as perfect when it comes to this," Maddie said. "There's just ... perfect for us."

Her eyes were glistening with unshed tears, and when Nick brushed the imaginary moisture away his face was unreadable. "What are you thinking right now?"

"Don't you know?"

"No. My heart is pounding so hard I can barely think at all. I want to know, though. I want to know everything you're thinking ... and feeling."

Maddie wet her lips. "I'm thinking that I never thought this would happen," she said. "I'm thinking that I don't deserve you. I'm thinking I've never been happier ... ever. I'm feeling ... nervous. My heart is pounding, too. My hands feel a little sweaty, and I'm worried I'm not going to live up to your expectations."

Maddie pressed her eyes shut, afraid to meet Nick's expressive eyes out of fear she would burst into tears and ruin the moment.

"There were times I worried this would never happen, too," Nick admitted. "I always believed ... deep down ... that you were my destiny. You deserve the very best in this world, Mad, and I'm not sure if I'm the very best, but I can promise you that no one will ever love you as much as I do."

The tears started to fall.

"I'm nervous, too," Nick said, wiping the tears away and pressing another kiss to her cheek. "You don't have to live up to anything. You're all I've ever wanted. You're all I'm ever going to want. This is new for both of us, and I want us to experience it all together.

"This is just the first time, Mad," he continued. "I think we both might have built it up to obscene proportions in our minds, and I'm desperate to make it perfect for you and you're terrified of letting me down. I think ... maybe ... we're both being a little ridiculous."

"I think so, too," Maddie admitted, her heart rolling. "I'm just ...

freaked out. I have no idea why. I've never trusted anyone more than you."

Nick chuckled. "I know the feeling. Here's the thing, Mad, I'm going to love you until the day I die. I've never loved anyone but you. This is just our next step. Are you ready to make it?"

"I've never been more ready."

Nick cupped Maddie's head and brought his lips to hers, the sensual kiss sending chills through her body as he rubbed her back. When they separated, Nick's face was a mask of emotion. "I love you, Maddie. I love you now, and I'm going to love you forever."

"I love you, too." Maddie choked on the words as the tears threatened to overtake her again. "You're my ... everything."

"Together we're everything," Nick said, getting to his feet. He leaned over and wrapped his arms around Maddie's body, hoisting her up and cradling her to his chest as he carried her back toward his bedroom. "I can't ever be without you again, Mad. It's you and me forever."

Maddie nodded, words failing her.

"Here we go, my Maddie."

**NICK** woke with a start, something yanking him out of the most peaceful slumber he'd ever experienced. The spot next to him in the bed was empty – and cold. *Where's Maddie?*

Nick scanned the dark room, cocking his head so he could listen to the sounds of the house. Was she in the bathroom? Something told him that wasn't the case. The house was too quiet. She wasn't inside. She was ... gone.

Nick's heart inadvertently flipped. He knew instinctively she wouldn't flee in the middle of the night. Something else had to be going on. He climbed out of the bed, grabbing his boxer shorts from the spot where he haphazardly discarded them hours before. He slipped into the boxers, and he was almost out of the bedroom before he noticed a hint of movement on the back deck. He stilled, and when the shadow on the lawn chair shifted again, Nick realized

Maddie hadn't disappeared – she'd just gone outside to enjoy the night.

Despite himself, Nick released a relieved sigh. He opened the door and let himself onto the deck silently, narrowing his eyes so he could focus on Maddie. Her hair was still in the ponytail, but it was mussed from some vigorous rolling around. It seemed – despite both their fears – some things did just come naturally. This was one of those things ... and Maddie had been wrong after all ... there was such a thing as perfection.

"What are you doing, Mad?" Nick asked the question quietly, hoping he wouldn't jolt her from whatever reverie she was living in as she stared at the sky.

"Did I wake you up?" Maddie asked, worried. The blanket from the chair next to his bed was wrapped around her naked body, and her bare shoulder was poking out.

"I think your absence in the bed woke me up," Nick said, unsure what was going on but determined to hear her out on her own terms. "Lean forward."

Maddie did as instructed, and Nick lifted her from the chair before settling himself in the warm seat – placing her on his lap and cuddling her close as he inhaled deeply. He wasn't sure what time it was, but it was clearly after midnight. The only sound intruding on their moment was that of the river down the way.

"I'm sorry you woke up without me," Maddie said, her voice small. "I ... I just wanted to come out here for a few minutes. I didn't think you would notice."

Nick's bravado at his earlier prowess was starting to slip. "Is something wrong? Did I ... do something?"

"No," Maddie said immediately, running her finger down his cheek. "I just ... I wanted to look at the stars."

Stargazing was one of their favorite activities. He understood the joy of a night sky. What he didn't understand was Maddie's need to leave him alone in bed after the best experience of his entire life. "You're worrying me a little bit," Nick admitted. "I can't help but feel I failed you somehow."

Maddie frowned. "Don't ever think that, Nicky," she said. "Nothing has ever been better than ... that. Nothing. I didn't even know it could be like that."

"Then what's wrong, Mad?"

"Nothing is wrong," Maddie said. "I'm just ... scared to fall asleep."

Nick stilled. "What?"

"I was laying there next to you thinking how I've never been happier in my whole life," Maddie said. "I could hear your heart beating, and your breath on my neck was warm and ... wonderful."

Nick waited.

"Then I started thinking that I might be dreaming," Maddie said. "I thought it was too perfect. I just knew it had to be a dream."

Nick's heart unclenched. "Oh, love."

"I wanted to get a little air and make sure I was really awake," Maddie explained. "I wanted to make sure it wasn't a dream. Then, well, I wanted to wait for a shooting star to wish upon. I thought if I could just see one ... then I'd know it was true. I'm scared to go to sleep and wake up and find this was all just the best dream I've ever had. It will crush me."

The hitch in his chest would have brought Nick to his knees if he'd been standing. "It wasn't a dream, my Maddie," he said. "It was just another step in our life together. I promise. When you wake up tomorrow, I'm going to be next to you. I'm going to be holding you."

"I know," Maddie said. "I just ... can we wait five minutes? I just want a shooting star. Just one. I'll give up after a few minutes."

Nick nodded, kissing her jaw lightly. "We can wait as long as you want." Since the blanket was drooping off of her shoulder, he reached over and pulled it back up. The idea that she was naked under the plush fabric was enticing ... but the knowledge that she needed a star to make this night perfect was more pressing. He closed his eyes and wished fervently. *Give her what she wants. No, give her what she needs.*

"There," Maddie said, shifting on his lap excitedly.

Nick opened his eyes and watched the bright streak of light as it shot across the horizon. He was relieved ... and empowered. He was starting to think he needed the star, too. "There's your proof, Mad."

"Make a wish."

Nick's mind wandered to a previous stargazing experience, one where he made a wish that didn't come true until a few hours before. He hadn't wished for sex then. He'd wished he'd have Maddie forever. It took more than ten years to come true, but it was well worth the wait.

"I've already gotten everything I've ever wished for, Mad," Nick said. "This is your star. You make the wish."

Maddie screwed her eyes shut, and Nick watched with unveiled marvel as his heart joined with hers in the unsaid wish. When she opened her eyes again she seemed more relaxed. "We can go to bed now."

"What did you wish for, Mad?"

"That every night for the rest of our lives would be just like this."

Nick smiled, tightening his arms around her as he lifted her and carried her back toward the bedroom. "Something tells me you're going to get what you wished for."

Her smile – and his happy heart – told him he was telling the truth. Sometimes wishes do come true.

## 9. NINE

Maddie woke the next morning to the most wonderful feeling ever – her naked body pressed tightly to Nick's as effervescent sun beckoned them through the flimsy bedroom curtains.

The urge to let loose with a lazy stretch called to her, but the idea of waking Nick was too much to bear. When she shifted her eyes so she could study his placid face her heart almost stopped. He was just so ... beautiful.

"I can feel you staring at me," Nick murmured.

Maddie sighed, frustrated. "I was trying to watch you sleep without waking you up. You look like one of those Greek statues. You're just so ... handsome."

Nick smiled, the expression turning his already chiseled face into something otherworldly. "I am handsome," he agreed. "You're beautiful, so that makes us a good match." He tightened his arm around her waist and pressed his lips to her forehead. "See, it wasn't a dream."

"Oh, it was a dream," Maddie said. "It was just the best dream ever. I never want to wake up."

Nick smiled, his eyes still shut. "Me either."

Maddie found she was a bundle of energy – and nerves – as she gazed up at Nick's strong jaw. "Nicky?"

"Hmm."

"What are you thinking?"

"I'm thinking I wish you would put your head back down on my chest and sleep for another hour."

Maddie frowned. "What else?"

Nick sighed, finally wrenching his eyes open and smiling at Maddie's lovely face. She looked so serious. "I'm thinking I love you."

"What else?"

*What was she looking for here?* Nick racked his brain. "I think I love the way your body feels against mine."

"What else?"

"Maddie, why don't you tell me what you're thinking and we'll go from there." Nick reached over and pushed the strands of blonde hair that dislodged from the ponytail overnight away from her face. "What's up?"

"I just want to know what you're feeling," Maddie said, averting her gaze. "I mean ... are you feeling happy?"

"Yes."

"Are you feeling ... comfortable?"

"Comfortable how? Are you asking if I like having your body pressed against mine? If so, yes. Never move it. Are you asking if I'm comfortable in this relationship? If so, yes. This is what I've always wanted. Either way, the answer is yes."

"So ... you're not going to get bored with me, right?"

Nick sighed, hating her worry. "Maddie?"

"What?"

"I can never get bored with you," Nick said. "Never. It can't happen. It's impossible. I'm not saying that to make you feel better. I'm saying it because it's the truth. You are it for me. You're the one. You're my forever. I don't care how insecure you get. Nothing is going to change that."

"Really?"

"Really."

Maddie lowered her head back to the spot above Nick's heart, loving the sound of its steady beat. "Yay."

Nick grinned as he rubbed the back of her head. "Yay," he agreed. "What are you thinking?"

"I'm debating if instigating another ... round ... would be too forward."

Nick stilled. "Excuse me?"

"I ... well ... I just want to see if it will be as good as the first time."

Nick's chest shook, laughter overtaking him. He forced Maddie's head up so he could meet her sea-blue eyes head on. "Love, if you ever think you're being too forward, take a step back and realize that if you climbed on top me every second for the rest of our lives I would die a happy man."

Maddie was hopeful. "Really?"

"You have no idea."

"Good," Maddie said, rolling on top of him and pressing her lips to his. "There's something I want to do."

"Those are the best words I've ever heard in my life. Buck up, little camper. I'm about to make your morning."

"**OKAY,** I've waited as long as I can, but we have to go to work."

John pushed Nick's bedroom door open, immediately wishing he'd had the forethought to knock. It was almost noon, but Maddie and Nick were still tangled together under the covers. Thankfully, they appeared to be sleeping.

Nick's eyes shot open, and he was aware enough of what was happening to tighten his arm around Maddie's bare back so she didn't expose herself to prying eyes as she attempted to bolt to a sitting position. "What are you doing?"

"I ... seriously ... you two are still in bed?"

"We had a long night," Nick said, rubbing Maddie's head to calm her. "What are you thinking just barging in here?"

"I didn't have much of a choice," John replied, nonplussed. "We're investigating a murder. I gave you guys as long as I could."

Nick sighed, resigned. "Go wait in the kitchen."

"But ... I haven't even had a chance to say hello to Maddie yet."

"Hi," Maddie said, her cheeks coloring. "It's good to see you."

"It's good to see you, too," John said. "How are things?"

"Good. Well ... perfect ... to be more precise."

John grinned. "It's about time. We've been waiting for this for what seems like forever."

"I think all of us have."

"Probably."

Nick growled. "Go into the kitchen, John," he ordered. "We're going to take a shower, and then we're going to be very excited by whatever breakfast you've cooked us."

"You're showering together? I don't have time to wait for that."

"Oh, you're going to wait," Nick snapped. "I ... just go out there. I'm going to beat you to within an inch of your life."

"You two look happy."

"We were ... until thirty seconds ago," Nick said.

"I'm still happy," Maddie said. "I'm a little embarrassed, though."

"Don't be," John said. "You look hot in the morning."

"I am going to kill you," Nick threatened.

"I'll cook your breakfast," John said. "You have twenty minutes. No ... funny stuff ... in the shower."

John shut the bedroom door, smiling when he heard Maddie dissolve into giggles as Nick softly swore, the heavy wood muting the angry words. He'd never seen his brother this happy. After ten years of misery, no one deserved that happiness more than Nick Winters. Now he just had to whip up a passable breakfast. They were probably starving.

**"WHAT** are we doing today?" Nick asked, grabbing a slice of bacon from Maddie's plate and chomping into it enthusiastically. "Did something happen this morning?"

"No," John said, using the spatula to give Maddie more scrambled eggs. "Eat your protein, honey. I think you need it with all the energy you've been expending."

Maddie smiled as her cheeks colored. "I ... thank you."

"You're making her feel uncomfortable," Nick scolded. "Don't you dare ruin this."

"I'm not trying to ruin this," John said, nonplussed. "Calm down. You're out of control. It's not necessary. I'm not trying to embarrass Maddie."

"I'm fine," Maddie said, forking into the eggs. "I really was hungry."

"Good," John said. "You're too thin."

"Leave her alone," Nick said, frustrated. "She's beautiful."

"Oh, she's stinking hot," John said. "I thought you were hot in high school, but you're even hotter now. It's ... amazing. My brother is a lucky man."

"I am," Nick agreed.

"I'm the lucky one," Maddie said. "He looks like an angel."

"He looks like a moron," John countered. "He's sloppy in love, and it makes him smile like he's got mental problems."

"You're lucky you're an only child," Nick said, focusing on Maddie. "You don't have to deal with this nonsense."

"I always wished I had a sister," Maddie said. "I thought ... well ... I thought it would finally give me someone female to talk to who wasn't my mother or grandmother."

Nick smirked. "You have Christy now."

"I do," Maddie agreed. "She's ... amazing."

"She *is* amazing," John said. "She's got a great personality – and her body isn't bad either."

Nick frowned. "Where did you sleep last night?"

"Don't worry about that."

"I am worried about that," Nick said. "Christy is a good person. Are you going to sleep with her and disappear?"

"Don't do that." Maddie shook her head for emphasis.

"First off, I didn't sleep with her last night," John said. "I thought about it. After my brother abandoned me to do ... whatever it is you two were doing until the wee hours of the morning ... I didn't have a lot of options."

"Christy is one of the best friends I've ever had," Maddie said, nervous. "She doesn't deserve for someone to sleep with and then abandon her."

"I just told you I didn't sleep with her," John said. "Calm down."

"Let's take this one step at a time," Nick said, placing his hand over Maddie's to still her. "Where did you sleep last night?"

"The dive on the highway that advertises free porn," John said. "Yes, that's their big claim to fame. You owe me."

"What happened after I left?"

"Are you asking if there was a catfight?"

"Why would there be a catfight?" Maddie asked, confused.

John furrowed his brow. "You didn't tell her? Shame on you."

Nick scowled. "I didn't want to upset her."

"It's too late for that," Maddie said, straightening in her chair. "What's going on?"

"I told you we went to the bar last night," Nick said. "I also told you we ran into Christy."

Maddie waited.

"What I didn't tell you is that we also ran into Marla and Cassidy."

Now it was Maddie's turn to scowl. "I ran into them yesterday, too."

"I heard," Nick said, moving his hand to the back of her head and pulling her closer so he could kiss her forehead. "Um ... thank you so much for this."

John refused to apologize. "You abandoned me."

"I left you with Christy," Nick said. "You two didn't even know I was in the same restaurant when I left."

"Tell me what happened with Marla and Cassidy," Maddie said, ignoring Nick's outburst.

"It wasn't anything big," Nick said. "Marla was ... well ... Marla."

"She always is. I don't really care about her. What happened with Cassidy?"

Nick narrowed his eyes. "I want to know what happened with you and Cassidy first."

Maddie took a sip of her coffee, stalling for time, and then she fixed an even look on Nick. "Marla accused me of being a homewrecker and Cassidy accused me of stealing the man that she loves. It was nothing new. What happened with you?"

"How upset were you?" Nick asked, ignoring the question.

"Not as upset as I would've been two weeks ago," Maddie admitted. "I'm done apologizing for being happy."

It was a reality Nick embraced weeks before, and he was so relieved Maddie was doing it now he almost wept. "Really?"

"I still feel bad for how Cassidy was hurt," Maddie cautioned. "I think we both could've handled that better."

"I agree," Nick said. "Well ... I agree on my part. I handled things just about as badly as any man could. You were nothing but respectful to her."

"She asked me how I felt about you when I first came back to town," Maddie countered. "Maybe not outright, but she was still trying to feel me out. She was insecure and worried. I told her we were just friends."

"We *were* just friends," Nick said. "You didn't lie to her."

"I knew I loved you," Maddie said. "I've always loved you. I've always known it, and I've always felt it. I knew the second I saw you again that I was still in love with you. It wasn't fair to lie to her."

Nick rubbed the heel of his palm against his forehead, annoyed. "Love, you weren't the one in a relationship even though you knew it wasn't going anywhere," he said. "I knew the second I saw you, too. I felt as if my heart was going to explode. I was already planning on walking away when you showed up. The only reason I didn't pull the trigger then was ... ." Nick broke off, unsure.

"Why?" John asked, curious. "Why didn't you end things then and make both of your lives easier?"

"At first I didn't want to do it because I knew everyone in town would jump to conclusions," Nick admitted. "I didn't want everyone naturally assuming I was dumping Cassidy for Maddie."

"Why?"

"Because I knew that certain people – that unholy wench, Marla, for example – would blame Maddie," Nick said. "Marla takes pleasure in making Maddie unhappy."

"I noticed that last night," John said. "She's ... awful."

"She's beyond awful," Nick said. "She's the Devil."

"I get that," John said. "What about after that? When did you finally acknowledge you wanted to be with Maddie?"

Nick balked. "I ... that's none of your business."

"I want to know, too," Maddie said. "I knew right away I was desperate to be with you. Sure, I didn't want to admit it, but Christy saw it. When did you know? And don't say something you think I want to hear. I want to know the truth."

Nick swallowed his upper lip with his lower, considering. "The first night we fell asleep in the window seat."

Maddie lifted her eyebrows, surprised. "Really?"

"Owning up to this in front of my brother, who is going to use it against me for the rest of my life, should prove how much I love you," Nick warned. "I don't want to hear another word about you worrying that I'm going to get bored with you."

It was a grand gesture, and Maddie considered it. "I agree to your terms."

Nick grinned. He couldn't help it. She was beautiful ... and she was happy. They both were happy. He was still going to pound his brother the first chance he got. "I felt as if our bodies just ... fit ... when I snuggled around you," he said. "It felt like ... coming home."

Maddie's angelic face brightened. "I felt the same way."

"I guess that's because we love each other," Nick said, leaning over so he could kiss her. "I knew at that moment that we were inevitable. That's when I had to start plotting how to break up with Cassidy without tipping off the whole town to what my intentions were."

"That didn't really work out so well, did it?" John asked.

"No," Nick said, rubbing his forehead. "I was going to tell her the night you almost drowned down at the lake." Nick internally cringed at the memory, flashes of breathing life back into Maddie's still lungs rendering him momentarily comatose.

Maddie gripped his hand tightly. "It doesn't matter. We're together now."

Nick regained his senses. "We are, my Maddie," he said, kissing her lightly. "We are."

"Now I'm definitely going to puke," John said.

Nick rolled his eyes. "What are we doing today?"

"We're going down to the pier to find Raymond Jacob Kingston."

"Why are you looking for him?" Maddie asked.

"Mildred says he's a pervert and we want to see if he knows anything about Hayley's death," Nick said. "I'm not sure how long I'll be, but I promise to call you when we're done."

"Screw that," Maddie said, hopping out of the chair. "I want to come."

Nick stilled. "You do?"

"I found Hayley's body," Maddie said, matter-of-fact. "We're in this together."

"Okay," Nick said. "You can come."

"She can?" John was surprised.

"She'll be able to help," Nick said. "Just ... you do what I tell you to do, Mad. That's the deal."

Maddie nodded. "I'm fine with that."

"What if I'm not fine with that?" John asked.

"You'll live," Nick said, unflappable. "Everyone be at the Explorer in five minutes."

Maddie smiled at John. "Shotgun."

"What is happening here?"

## 10. TEN

"I'm going to walk around," Maddie said, her gaze bouncing around the pier. "Text me when you guys are done looking for Raymond."

Nick grabbed Maddie's arm before she could walk off. "What?"

"I'm going to walk around."

"Why?"

"I ... just want to look around."

Nick scowled. "Why did you come with us if you want to wander off on your own?"

"I didn't think it was a big deal," Maddie replied, confused. "If you don't want me to go ... I won't go."

"What is your deal?" John asked. "It's the pier. Do you think someone is going to grab her?"

Nick stilled, unsure how to answer. That was exactly what he was worried about. Now that he had her, the idea of losing Maddie was crippling. Internally, he knew she'd managed to live ten years of her life without him. Deep down, though, he was terrified something would happen and snatch his happiness away. "I ... of course not." Nick released his grip on Maddie's arm. "Please don't go too far."

Maddie pressed her lips together. "I can sit here if you want."

John glanced between his brother and Maddie. "What's going on?"

"Nothing," Nick said, averting his gaze. "I just ... can't stand to be away from her if I don't have to." He leaned forward and kissed Maddie. "I love you."

"I love you, too," Maddie said. She leaned in so only he could hear her next words. "No one will take me from you."

Nick hugged her briefly. "I know. We'll be here. Look around. See if ... you can find anything."

"I will." Maddie plastered a bright smile on her face when she turned to John. "Take care of my man."

"You two are cute," John said.

"Thank you."

"You're also weird."

"Thank you."

John scowled. "I'm going to find out what's going on here."

"You're not that good of a cop," Nick said. "Don't go far, Mad. We'll all get lunch together in two hours."

"You guys just ate," John complained.

Nick ignored him. "Two hours, love."

Maddie nodded. "Okay."


**BLACKSTONE** Pier was one of those places Maddie loved in theory but didn't enjoy in practice. She was infatuated with the lake, especially the wind whipping her hair over the choppy water. What she didn't enjoy was the smell. She loved fishing – there was something soothing about the entire endeavor – but she didn't love the end olfactory product. It often made her queasy. For some reason, the scents of the pier almost always overpowered her.

"You look like you're going to pass out."

Maddie lifted her head, smiling at Mildred's concerned face. "Hi, Mildred. It's so good to see you."

"It's good to see you, too, girlie," Mildred said. "What's up with your life?"

Of all her grandmother's friends, Mildred was one of Maddie's favorites. She was one of the only people who didn't put up with Maude's outrageous shenanigans and just go along blindly when she proposed a plan. "My life is good."

"I can see that," Mildred said, looking Maddie up and down with a steady gaze. "You were always a pretty girl, but you're practically glowing now. I'm guessing I lost the sex pool."

"You were part of that pool, too?"

"Boredom is a funny thing," Mildred said. "I had my eye on a new fishing pole. I guess Maude won this one. Did she lock you in a room together and confiscate your clothes? That's what she was threatening."

"No," Maddie said, shaking her head. "I ... I can't talk about this."

"You always were a sweet girl."

"I don't know about that," Maddie said. "I'm just ... embarrassed."

"Honey, that Winters boy grew up to look like a model," Mildred said. "In fact, you grew up to look like a model, too. You're beautiful apart, but you're breathtaking together."

"I didn't know you had the soul of a poet," Maddie teased.

"I don't," Mildred replied, nonplussed. "I just know the truth when I see it. You're happy. It looks good on you."

"Thank you."

Mildred rolled her eyes. "If you're going to get all emotional, I'm leaving now."

"Don't leave yet," Maddie said, collecting herself. "I have a few questions for you first."

"I'm waiting."

"I want to talk about Hayley Walker."

Mildred frowned. "The dead girl? I guess that shouldn't surprise me. Are you out here with your boyfriend?"

"He's here," Maddie said. "I'm asking for myself, though."

"I didn't know the girl very well," Mildred said. "I did see her down here on occasion."

Maddie recognized the disapproving tilt of Mildred's head. "What was she doing?"

"At first, I thought she was a shy girl who was just trying to make friends. That impression didn't last long."

Maddie waited.

"After a few weeks, I started to realize she was boy crazy," Mildred said.

"What do you mean?"

"The first few weeks she sat on the benches and worked on her homework," Mildred said. "It was nice to see. Most of the kids these days have their faces glued to their cell phones."

"They do."

"After a few weeks, though, there was less studying of the books and more studying of the boys."

"Do you know which boys?"

Mildred shrugged. "I'm not good with the teenage gossip. I do know she often talked to the Jarvis boy. He works at the food truck during the summer."

Maddie racked her brain. "Michael Jarvis?"

Mildred nodded.

"He would be Pamela and Drew Jarvis' boy, right? I babysat him when he was really little a couple of times. What can you tell me about him?"

"The boy is a poof."

A poof? *Uh-oh.* "Just for clarification, what do you mean by that?"

"He's a homosexual," Mildred said. "That's what it means when you call someone a poof."

Maddie tried to ignore the derogatory comment. "What makes you think he was gay?"

"He spent all his time checking out the other boys when he thought no one was looking."

"What about the girls?"

"He talked to them," Mildred replied, shrugging. "He never paid any of them attention. He really only talked to Hayley. They seemed pretty tight."

"And you're sure they weren't flirting, right?"

"I know what flirting looks like," Mildred said. "I haven't done it in decades, but I still remember what it looks like. The times may change, but human behavior doesn't."

Maddie couldn't argue with that. "Tell me about Raymond Jacob Kingston."

"He's a pervert."

"I've heard," Maddie said, keeping her voice even. "Give me some specifics."

"He stares at the young girls and makes lewd comments."

"What do the girls do?"

"They point and laugh."

"How does Raymond take that?"

Mildred seemed surprised by the question. "He acts like it's fine most of the time."

"What about the other times?"

"I can tell it bothers him."

Maddie pursed her lips, thinking. "Do you think Raymond is capable of killing someone?"

"I don't know," Mildred said. "He seems like one of those dirty old men who is all talk and no action, but there's still something ... off ... about him."

"Have you seen him?"

"I told your boyfriend I would call if I did."

"Keep your eyes open," Maddie said. "I'm not saying Raymond is a murderer, but Hayley Walker was a teenage girl and whoever killed her is ... ."

"A monster?"

"That's too nice of a word," Maddie said. "Just keep your eyes open and be careful. This world would be a sad place without you."

"The same can be said about you, Maddie Graves," Mildred said. "You were a beautiful child, and one of the few teenagers who didn't make me want to kill someone. It looks to me as if you've grown into a pretty good woman. This world would be a sad place without you."

. . .

"WHAT'S going on with you and Maddie?" John asked, scanning the myriad of faces for an unfamiliar one to question.

"We're happy."

"Not that," John said. "Why is she here?"

Nick shifted uncomfortably. "I just want to be close to her."

John's eyes were probing as they rested on his youngest sibling. "I know something else is going on here. You were scared to let her wander off on her own. I want to know why."

"She has an unnatural knack for finding trouble," Nick replied, honest. "She's been back in town for two months and she's almost been killed twice."

John chuckled. "Have you ever considered that was just bad luck?"

"No," Nick said. "Todd picked her out on purpose. He was going to ... do terrible things to her."

"And the former mayor? Why did he zero in on her?"

That was a prickly question. "I don't know," Nick lied. "Maybe it was because she stopped him from killing Tara the first time."

"I kind of heard about that," John said carefully. "Did she really throw shoes at him?"

"She didn't know what else to do."

"Did she really fall off the curb and injure her ankle?"

Nick growled. "Yes."

"Do you really wish you were still in bed with her and I would stop asking you annoying questions?"

Nick's face softened. "Yes."

"I'm sorry," John said. "I didn't want to bother you. I knew you two were ... having the time of your life. How was it, by the way?"

"I'm still not talking about it with you," Nick said. "I don't kiss and tell."

"You've been smiling since I barged into your bedroom," John said. "Sure, you keep giving me dirty looks, but every time you talk about Maddie ... or think about Maddie ... you smile."

"She makes me smile."

"She does," John said. "You make her smile, too."

"I certainly hope so."

"I still think there's something going on," John said, his eyes glued to Nick's face. "Tell me what it is."

Nick ignored him, refusing to make eye contact. "Look."

John was reticent, but he finally shifted his eyes and focused on the man Nick was pointing toward. "What am I looking at?"

"I think that's Raymond."

John instantly sobered. "How well do you know him?"

"Just by his face," Nick replied. "I'm not sure I've ever spoken to him."

John studied the man. "He looks ... ."

"He's not homeless," Nick said. "He has an apartment in that big building on Plum Street."

"I was going to say he looks dirty," John said. "How often do you think he showers?"

"He likes to fish," Nick said, moving forward. "Fishing is a dirty business." Nick didn't give his brother a chance to respond, instead approaching the man slowly, his hand outstretched. "Mr. Kingston?"

Kingston's eyes flashed to Nick, and it appeared as if it took him a moment to focus. "Do I know you?"

Nick flashed his badge. "I'm with the Blackstone Bay Police Department."

"You're the Winters boy."

"Yes, that's me. I have a few questions for you."

"About?"

"About a dead girl who washed up on shore the other day," Nick said. "I ... ."

He never got a chance to finish his sentence. Kingston tilted his head to the side, giving all appearances that he was listening and then bolted down the pier the second Nick relaxed.

"What the ... ?"

"That's a great interrogation method," John said.

"I ... come on." Nick broke into a run, racing after Kingston. The man was in his seventies. Even with a head start he couldn't outrun the fit Winters brothers.

"Let's make a game of it," John said, increasing his pace so he was slightly in front of Nick. "If I catch him, you have to give me ten thousand bucks off the house."

Nick glowered. "And if I win?"

"I nail Christy tonight."

Nick faltered. "I ... ."

"Let me win and Christy is safe," John said.

Nick hated the suggestion, the idea of losing a footrace to his brother going against his basic nature. The thought of Maddie's heart breaking because Christy was hurting was too much to bear, though. Nick eased up on his stride. "Go ahead and get him."

John was surprised by Nick's concession. "You're just giving up?"

"He's seventy," Nick said. "If you can't catch him ... you're not much of a cop."

John frowned but increased his pace, finishing with a burst as Kingston closed in on the sandy beach – and potential freedom. He launched himself into the air, landing on the man and tackling him to the ground with an impressive thud.

Nick fought the urge to both applaud and laugh. "Were you channeling your days from the football team?"

John ignored him, easily holding Kingston down on the ground as he tried to buck up and dislodge him. "I won."

"You did," Nick agreed. "Don't you dare hurt Christy."

"Why do you care?"

"She's been wonderful with Maddie," Nick replied. "She won't let her feel sorry for herself and she's been great with her self-esteem. She's a very good woman."

"I like her."

"You're not ready to settle down," Nick said. "You're a good man, but Christy deserves someone who is willing to settle down."

John sighed. "Fine. I want you to know that I'm giving up something really good here to keep your girlfriend happy, though."

"I know," Nick said. "Thank you."

"You're welcome." John glanced down at Kingston, whose face

was just about as red as it could get. "Are you ready to answer some questions?"

"I'm not talking to you," Kingston spat. "You're the man. I don't talk to the man."

"Great," John said. "He's paranoid."

"I think he just doesn't like you."

"I have that effect on some people," John lamented. "I can't explain it."

"Let me try," Nick said, hunkering down so he could meet Kingston's fervent gaze. "Will you talk to me?"

"You look like the jackhole that tackled me."

"Is that a no?"

"That's a no," Kingston said. "I'm not talking to anyone."

Maddie picked that moment to reappear. "What's going on?"

Nick smiled at her, loving the way the sun glinted off her flaxen hair. "Hello, my Maddie. What have you been doing?"

"Talking to Mildred."

"She's fun," Nick said.

"She is," Maddie agreed, glancing at John's captive. "What's going on?"

"I let my brother catch him in exchange for not breaking Christy's heart," Nick said. "I want points."

"You can have all the points in the world."

Nick wrinkled his nose, fighting the urge to kiss her. "I love you."

"I love you."

"I'm going to puke," John said, grappling with Kingston to keep him contained. "You two are sickening."

Kingston finally focused his attention on Maddie. "Hello, beautiful."

"Hi," Maddie said, smiling. "Are you in pain?"

"Honey, I hurt the second you fell from Heaven and landed on me."

Maddie faltered. "I'm not sure I understand."

"He's saying you look like an angel, Mad," Nick supplied.

"Oh, well, thank you."

Kingston grinned. "You're really pretty."

"She's also really taken," Nick said. "Don't even think of saying anything lewd to her. I hear you're a pervert, and she's already spoken for."

"I'm not a pervert."

"You look like a pervert," John said.

"I'm not the one rubbing his junk against another man," Kingston said.

John balked. "I ... don't be gross. Are you ready to answer some questions?"

Kingston tilted his head to the side, considering. "I'm not answering any questions you ask."

"Great."

"I will let the blonde question me, though."

Nick and John exchanged a look.

"No way," Nick said.

"We'll be right here."

"I ... ."

"I'll ask him some questions," Maddie said, brightening. "I'll be the good cop."

Nick's face softened. "You're the good everything, love."

"Yup, I'm definitely going to puke," John said.

## 11. ELEVEN

"Can I get you something to make you more comfortable?" Maddie asked, sitting down at one of the metal bistro tables in front of the food truck and shooting Kingston a small smile.

John and Nick positioned themselves on either side of the man – just in case he tried to run or go after Maddie – but were otherwise silent.

"I want a hamburger and a Coke," Kingston said. "I need fuel after this ... ogre ... tackled me and hurt my knee."

"You shouldn't have run," John said.

"You shouldn't have chased me."

"I wouldn't have chased you if you hadn't run," John said.

"I wouldn't have run if you hadn't chased me."

This was getting them nowhere. "Raymond, hey, can you look at me?" Maddie tapped the tabletop for emphasis, studying Kingston's heavily lined face. His complexion was sallow, his eyes furtive as he cast occasional glances in John's direction. If Maddie had to guess, she was fairly sure Kingston was getting most of his nutrients out of a bottle these days.

"I like looking at you," Kingston said, shooting her a grin that had a few gaps in it. "You're pretty."

"Thank you," Maddie said.

"You're really hot."

"Thank you."

"Would you like me to help you bait your hook?"

Nick growled. "She can bait her own hook."

John snickered at the double entendre while Maddie's cheeks burned. "Nice, bro."

Nick glared at him. "Shut up."

Maddie fought to retain her calm demeanor. "Raymond, no one wants to accuse you of anything you didn't do," she said. "We're just looking for some information. If you answer our questions truthfully, I'm sure you'll be on your way relatively quickly."

Kingston didn't look convinced. "What makes you say that?"

"I have faith," Maddie said. "Now, Nick here is going to get your hamburger and Coke, and we're just going to talk."

"Wait a second ... ."

Maddie held up her hand to quiet Nick. "Please?"

He sighed. There was no way he could deny her, especially when she was going out of her way to make all of their lives easier. "I'm only going to be three feet over there," Nick said, pointing. "Don't say anything ... untoward ... to my girlfriend. I'm not going to like it."

"Hey, she's an adult," Kingston said, his eyes twinkling. "She can choose a man for herself. I might be more her speed."

Maddie made a face while Kingston was focused elsewhere, and Nick fought the mad urge to laugh because she was so adorable. "You're right, Raymond," Nick said. "If you can steal my Maddie from me, I guess you deserve her." He winked at Maddie. "Try to contain yourself, love. You're going to break my heart."

Maddie grinned. "I'll do my best."

Nick got up from the table and wandered over to the food truck to order Kingston's food. He kept his ears on the conversation while he leaned against the truck to wait for the order.

"Tell me about Hayley Walker, Raymond," Maddie prodded. "I heard you talked to her a few times."

"I'm not sure which girl that is," Kingston said.

"She was young. She had blonde hair, although it was darker than mine ... and shorter. She had big green eyes, and she often wore hoodies and blue jeans. Mildred says she sat on that bench right over there and worked on her homework a lot of the time."

Nick frowned. Mildred hadn't told him that. Of course, Maddie had a way with people. She could get them to open up without even trying sometimes.

"Was she the one who always had real books?" Kingston asked.

Maddie nodded. "Mildred says she was different from the other teenagers down here because she didn't spend all of her time on her cell phone."

"I remember her," Kingston said. "She was quiet and kept to herself ... except for some of the teenage boys. I would see her talking to them sometimes."

"That's what Mildred said," Maddie said. "Do you remember which boys you saw her talking to?"

Kingston shrugged. "All of the boys look the same to me."

"That's because you only like the girls, isn't it?" John asked.

"It would be unnatural for me to like the boys," Raymond replied, nonplussed. "I'm not one of *those* guys."

"Who are *those* guys?" Maddie asked.

"You know the ones," Kingston said. "They're the ones who shave their chests and wax their eyebrows and smell like they're wearing perfume ... like these two."

Maddie pressed her lips together to keep from laughing out loud. "Like these two?"

"They're clearly *that* way." Kingston waggled his eyebrows.

"They're brothers," Maddie said.

"That makes it grosser."

"Okay," Nick said, nodding at the woman behind the counter as she handed him the hamburger and Coke. "That will be enough of that." He slid the food items in front of Kingston.

Kingston dug into the hamburger enthusiastically. "If you want to hide who you are, I encourage it," he said. "I would hide it, too."

"Thank you," Nick said, moving to the spot behind Maddie and resting his hand on her shoulder. "Answer the rest of Maddie's questions."

Kingston nodded happily. "I said I would."

"When was the last time you saw Hayley?" Maddie asked, hoping to get the conversation back on track.

"I have no idea," Kingston replied. "The days kind of meld together for me. That's what happens when you retire."

"Do you remember the last time you saw her?"

"Yeah," Kingston said, wiping the corner of his mouth with the sleeve of his shirt. "She was sitting on that bench and she was having an argument with the boy who works at the food truck."

"Michael Jarvis?"

Kingston nodded. "He's like these two."

"Is he saying he's gay?" John asked.

Maddie nodded.

"Is he really gay, or is he gay like we are?" Nick asked.

"I have no idea," Maddie said. "Mildred said he was a ... poof. I'm not sure it matters."

"It opens up the suspect pool if she was down here visiting Michael all of the time," Nick said. "If he really is gay, that shifts his motivations."

"Meaning they wouldn't be sexual," Maddie mused, rubbing the back of her neck.

Nick pushed her hand away and dug in with his own fingers, massaging her absentmindedly. "Raymond, you didn't hurt Hayley, did you?"

"Of course not," Kingston said. "I keep to myself. I would never hurt someone."

"Then why did you run?" John asked.

"When the cops come after you it's hard to calm yourself down long enough to think," Kingston said. "It just seemed like the right thing to do."

John shifted his attention to Nick. "What do you think?"

Nick tilted his head to the side, considering. "I ... ."

Instinctively Maddie reached across the table and clamped her hand around Kingston's wrist, closing her eyes briefly. After about ten seconds, she released her grip. "I believe you, Raymond," she said. "You need to lay off the drinking, though, and a shower wouldn't hurt you."

Kingston smirked. "Thanks for the tip."

"I'M NOT sure we should've just let him go," John said.

After another two hours of questions and people watching, and no forward momentum, Maddie, Nick and John decided to call it an afternoon. The three of them were at one of the local restaurants, Maddie snuggled in at Nick's side on one side of the booth, and John spread out on the other.

"He's not guilty," Maddie said.

"You don't know that," John said. "Just because he says he's not guilty, that doesn't mean he's telling the truth."

"We don't have any evidence to haul him in," Nick said. "We have no reason to suspect him. Just because everyone thinks he's a pervert, that doesn't mean he did anything perverted to Hayley. The coroner couldn't say with any certainty whether she was sexually assaulted. The water made it impossible to ascertain whether or not she had sexual contact before her death."

"We could've taken him in because he fled from law enforcement," John said. "That would get him off the streets until we find out the truth."

"He's harmless," Maddie said. "He likes to talk big. That doesn't make him a bad guy."

"And you figured that all out just by touching him?" John asked, arching an eyebrow.

Maddie stilled. "I ... I just feel it."

"No, you put your hand on him and then decided he was innocent," John said. "Is this part of that whole psychic thing you do?"

Maddie's face drained of color, her heart pounding. "What?"

"What are you talking about?" Nick asked, edgy.

"I know you're psychic, Maddie," John said. "I want to know what you saw when you touched him. Did you see his future? His past?"

Maddie's face was awash with fear and betrayal when she shifted her gaze to Nick. "Y-y-you told him?"

"No," Nick said, immediately shaking his head. "I would never ... ."

Maddie started to slide out of the booth, evading Nick's hand as he extended it and tried to grab her wrist. "I have to go to the bathroom."

"Mad ... ."

"It's fine. I just ... have to go to the bathroom." Maddie averted her eyes from John as she tried to collect herself. "Everything is ... fine. I'll be back in a few minutes."

Nick watched her go, worried. Once he was sure she was out of earshot he turned on his brother. "Who told you that?"

John placed his tongue in his cheek, unsure how to proceed. Maddie's reaction wasn't what he expected. "I just figured it out on my own."

"How?"

"There were always rumors about Olivia," John said. "There were a lot of rumors about Maddie when you guys were kids, too. I ignored most of them. I just ... it kind of made sense. She was a skittish kid. When she came back she was in the middle of two murder investigations. Then there's you."

"Me?"

"You're very protective of her," John said.

"I love her."

"It's more than that," John said. "You didn't want her wandering off on her own. You were perfectly fine with her questioning Kingston. You believed her without a second thought when she said Kingston was innocent after touching him."

Nick shook his head, pushing the heel of his hand against his forehead as he thought. "Why would you possibly just blurt it out like that? Why did you do that?"

"I didn't think it was a big deal," John said. "You obviously know.

You wouldn't tell me why she left when you were teenagers. Everything just kind of came together this afternoon. I honestly didn't think she would react like that."

"She's scared," Nick hissed. "Olivia told her people would turn on her if they knew what she could do."

"What can she do?"

"It doesn't matter," Nick said. "Don't ever talk to her about it again, and don't you dare tell anyone."

John held his hands up, surprised at his brother's vehemence. "I didn't mean to upset her. I get it."

"You don't get anything," Nick said. "You have no idea what she's been through. I don't even know everything she's been through."

"What is that supposed to mean?"

"None of your business," Nick said, furrowing his brow. "It doesn't matter."

"It obviously matters to you."

"Maddie didn't want to tell me what was going on when she came back," Nick said. "She was terrified I would turn on her. She thought ... she thought I would walk away out of shame or disgust."

"I get that," John said. "You obviously didn't, though."

"Nothing will drive me away from her," Nick said. "I don't care what she can do. I love who she is."

"Ah, we're back to the poetry."

Nick made a face. "When I was trying to figure out why she would be at a murder scene in the middle of the night I ran her name through the system and came up with multiple hits in police files down by Detroit."

John waited, curious.

"I called the detective in all of the files," Nick said. "He wouldn't say a lot. What he did say is Maddie helped him find several missing people, including children."

"That's good," John said. "She's obviously good at what she does."

"He also said that whatever her last case was, it went bad," Nick said. "She didn't help him again, and whatever it was ... scarred her. She doesn't want to talk about it."

"Maybe you should make her talk about it," John suggested.

"When she's ready, she'll talk," Nick said. "You can't push her."

"I wasn't trying to push her," John protested. "I'm sorry. I didn't realize it was going to be such a big deal."

Nick pinched the bridge of his nose and then started to climb out of the booth. "I need to talk to her."

"Do you want me to wait here?" John asked.

"That would be great," Nick sneered. When he started moving toward the back of the restaurant the waitress who had taken their orders stopped him. "Are you leaving, too?"

"Too?"

"The blonde woman who was with you left a few minutes ago," the waitress said. "I just want to know if you want me to cancel your orders."

The color drained from Nick's face. "My brother will be paying. Did you see which way she went when she left?"

The waitress shrugged. "If you want to wait, I'll be done with my shift in two hours. I would never leave a guy like you behind."

Nick scowled. "Thanks for the generous offer. I'm a one-woman guy, though, and I've already got my woman."

Now he just had to find her.

## 12. TWELVE

Maddie's head was busy as she left the restaurant, purposely turning away from the parking lot and heading toward the pier. She didn't know why she was running, only that she needed air.

John calling her out on being psychic jolted her. There was no other way to put it. She'd been at the height of happiness until then, her life finally how she wanted it. Now she felt like she was choking.

Her mother ingrained the dangers of telling people about her "peculiarity" from the moment Maddie started manifesting powers. She knew she was never to trust anyone other than Olivia and Maude. That's what she always believed, and that was the decision that ultimately propelled her out of Blackstone Bay as a teenager. The last thing she'd wanted to do was leave Nick, and only Olivia's death had the emotional strength to bring her back.

When Nick figured out her secret, he'd been mad at himself for not realizing sooner. He said the pieces were there, he'd just never managed to put the puzzle together. Instead of reacting with anger, he'd embraced her and reiterated that it didn't matter. The love he expressed that afternoon wasn't of the romantic kind, but it was the kind that filled her heart and lifted her.

She was having trouble reconciling that memory with the knowledge that Nick told his brother her secret. *He didn't. He wouldn't. He would never betray me.* Maddie knew that instinctively. John found out some other way.

So why had she slipped out of the restaurant? Maddie didn't have an answer for that other than she needed a few moments to collect herself. She reached to her side, searching for her purse so she could send Nick a text message and tell him she was okay. He was probably in the midst of a righteous meltdown right about now, worry over her overtaking him. Unfortunately, she'd left her purse back at the restaurant. It was in the booth next to John.

"Crap," Maddie muttered.

"You know they say talking to yourself is a sign of mental unbalance."

Maddie shifted when she heard the voice, fear washing over her momentarily until she focused on the craggy face watching her from a few feet away.

"Are you all right, girl? You look like you've seen a ghost."

Maddie laughed hollowly, the joke hitting home. "I've seen my fair share."

The man was dressed in simple jeans and a T-shirt, a fishing pole in his hand and one of those canvas hats with a myriad of lures tacked to it perched on top of his head. He looked to be in his sixties, his green eyes kind as they looked her up and down. "Do you need help?"

Maddie pressed her lips together, running a hand through her hair as she tried to steady herself. "I don't suppose you have a cell phone, do you?"

"Sorry," the man said. "I never carry one. I don't see the need. The only person I need to call is my brother, and we don't have much to say to one another."

"I'm Maddie Graves," Maddie said, straightening as she introduced herself. "I'm sorry to ruin your evening. I know that afternoon fishermen take their task very seriously."

The man extended his hand. "I'm David Crowder. No offense,

girlie, but you don't look like the type of woman who spends a lot of time fishing."

"I think you just insulted me," Maddie said, smiling for real this time. "I'll have you know I'm an expert fisherwoman."

David looked dubious. "Where's your gear?"

"I'm not fishing right now," Maddie explained. "I was having dinner with some friends and ... well ... I had a little bit of a meltdown and had to leave. I don't think it was one of my prouder moments."

"Don't worry about it," David said, waving his hand. "As you get older you'll realize you care less and less about what people think about you and more and more about what you think about yourself."

"That's good advice. What do you think of yourself?"

"I'm a simple guy who likes to fish," David said. "I'm pretty much an open book. What do you see when you look at yourself?"

Maddie shrugged. "Sometimes I think I see a good person. Sometimes I think I see a strong person. I rarely see the person I want to see."

"That's a comment on your age, not how good you are," David said, winding his reel. "When you're young you always want to better yourself. You don't see your good points. Don't worry. I have a feeling other people see your good points."

*Like Nick*, Maddie said silently. All he saw was her good points. "You're sweet," Maddie said. "Can I ask why you're out here at this time of day? I thought the best time to fish was after midnight and before dawn. You have a few hours left before the fish really start biting."

"I come out here quite often when the weather allows," David said.

"You're not married?"

"She died last year."

Maddie's heart rolled. "I'm so sorry. That was insensitive. I shouldn't have asked. It's none of my business."

"It doesn't matter," David said. "It is what it is."

"I'm still sorry."

"What about you? Where is your husband? Does he allow you to wander around the pier with a bunch of crude fishermen all the time, or is this just a special occasion?"

Maddie smirked. "I'm not married."

"You have a special someone, though," David said. "I could tell that when I first saw you. That's what has you upset."

"I'm not sure I'm upset," Maddie said. "I think I was upset ... and then I realized I had nothing to be upset about. Then I was upset with myself for being upset."

"That's some convoluted thinking, missy."

"It is," Maddie agreed. She gestured toward the end of David's hook and the brightly colored lure hanging there. "May I?"

David nodded, watching as Maddie delicately fingered the pink feathers. "You made this yourself."

"How can you tell?"

"The stitching is strong but not straight," Maddie said. "You can tell you put your heart into it. You can't say the same thing about store-bought lures."

"Be careful," David warned. "If you touch a man's lure like that, people will begin to talk."

"I guess," Maddie said, taking a step back. "Thank you for being so nice to me. You didn't have to. Most people would've written me off as a crazy woman. I should probably get back to my boyfriend, though. He's probably going nuts."

David inclined his head toward a spot behind Maddie. "I wouldn't worry about it. I think he's coming this way now."

Maddie swiveled quickly, relief flooding her when she caught sight of Nick. He hadn't seen her yet, and when his gaze landed on her he broke into a jog. "Are you okay?"

Maddie let him gather her into his arms, his face nestling in her hair as he rubbed her back. "I'm sorry. I shouldn't have left. I just ... ."

"I know, Mad," Nick said, kissing her cheek. "I know why you were upset. It's still not okay to scare me."

"I'm sorry."

Nick cupped the back of her head, tilting her face up so he could study it. She didn't look like she'd been crying, and her color was good. He'd been imagining any number of horrible scenarios when he couldn't find her outside of the restaurant. "We need to have a talk here, Mad," Nick said, smiling at David tightly as he pulled away slightly. "I need you to know that I didn't tell my brother ... anything."

"I know that."

"Are you sure? You didn't seem to know that in the restaurant."

"I did know it in the restaurant. I just didn't know I knew it. Does that make sense?"

Nick's face softened. "I guess. I would never ... ."

"I know. I'm sorry." Maddie wrapped her arms around Nick's waist, resting her head on his shoulder as he tightened his arms around her. "I'm so sorry."

"I love you, Maddie," Nick murmured, rocking her slightly.

"See, I knew you were having man trouble," David said.

Nick lifted his eyes to meet David's serious countenance. "Is that what she told you? Did she say she was having man trouble?"

"She said she thought she was upset and then realized she wasn't upset so she became upset about getting upset," David said. "She's a woman. They have convoluted minds."

Nick smirked. "They do. Thank you for watching over her. I couldn't imagine my life without her."

"Something tells me that's not going to be a problem," David said. "You might want to keep a closer eye on her, though, especially after they found that girl's body down the beach."

"That's a pretty good point," Nick said. "Speaking of that, I happen to be an officer with the Blackstone Bay Police Department. You didn't know the victim, did you? Did you ever see her down here?"

"I don't think so," David said. "I don't hang out here much during the day, and that's when the teenagers tend to be here."

"That makes sense," Nick said. "Just do me a favor and keep your ears to the ground. If you hear anyone talking about Hayley Walker ... or anything that sounds suspicious ... call us."

"I'll do that," David said. "You'll have to do me a favor in return, though."

Nick waited.

"Watch that girl," David said. "She's clearly your whole world. You're going to find that when your world dies, you don't have a lot to live for. Try to make sure you hold on to your world for as long as you can."

Nick held Maddie flush against his chest. "I'll never let her go."

"Well ... don't go all stalker or anything," David said. "Women don't like that."

Nick barked out a laugh. "Thanks for the tip."

**"WHERE** is John?" Maddie asked, her fingers linked with Nick's as he led her down the pier.

"He's probably eating his dinner," Nick said. "I left him there with three dishes and a bill."

"I'm so ... ."

"Don't finish that sentence, Mad," Nick said. "I know you were upset, and John saying what he did threw you. It threw me, too."

"Did he say where he heard it?"

"He said he figured it out on his own," Nick said. "He heard the rumors ... and he thought I was being hyper vigilant ... and he knew about your mom. I told him not to bring it up again."

"It's okay," Maddie said. "He's your brother. I trust him."

"Maddie, I don't want you to feel shame about this," Nick said, his eyes somber. "You're amazing. You're the most amazing person I've ever known. What you can do is a miracle. I understand wanting to keep it a secret but never doubt that I love you ... or that I'm proud of you."

Maddie bit her lower lip. "I love you, too."

"Good," Nick said. "You were going to ruin my night if you didn't say it back."

His grin was so lazy Maddie couldn't help but laugh. "You think you're pretty charming, don't you?"

"I have my moments," Nick said. "Now, come on, love. You need food. We have to talk about the case with John for a little bit and then we're going back to my house."

"We are?"

"I have plans for you." Nick winked.

"No, you don't," Maddie said, internally grinning as Nick's smile faltered. "I have plans for you."

"Ah, I stand corrected." Nick pulled Maddie's hand up and brushed his lips across the ridge of her knuckles. "You'd better eat a lot. I have a feeling your plans are going to tire you out."

"Do you think John is still here? I left my purse in the booth next to him, by the way. I hope he hasn't left."

"He hasn't," Nick said, pointing. "His truck is still here. We'll get some food, John will apologize, and then we'll go home. I want to spend some time with just you."

"All this time you're spending with me isn't impacting your work, is it?"

"Life is hard," Nick said. "We'll make it work. I'm not cutting my time with you and I'm not giving up on this case, so I guess you're going to have to work with me."

"Oh, that sounds fun."

Nick and Maddie walked back into the restaurant, pulling up short when they saw John was still in the booth. He wasn't alone, though.

"You've got to be kidding me," Nick said. "How did she even know we were here?"

Maddie shrugged, a wide smile splitting her face when she caught sight of Christy. "I have no idea, but I'm glad to see her."

"Why?"

"She's one of the few other people who knows my secret and doesn't judge me," Maddie said. "It might make things easier when I talk to your brother."

"You don't have to talk to him if you don't want to."

"I want to," Maddie said. "He's your family."

"You're my family. He's just the kid who used to give me wedgies when I was little."

They were bold words, but Maddie knew they weren't true. Nick loved his brother, and that meant Maddie was going to have to smooth things over if they all wanted to be happy – and she desperately wanted Nick to be happy. She wanted them both to be happy ... together.

## 13. THIRTEEN

"Are we interrupting something?" Nick asked, his gaze bouncing between Christy and John.

"Of course not," Christy said, smiling brightly. "I just happened to stop in for some dinner and saw John sitting here alone. I didn't realize you guys were here, too."

"I wasn't sure if you were coming back," John said, his dark eyes fixed on Maddie. "I'm really sorry."

"It's fine," Maddie said. "I overreacted. I do that sometimes."

"It's not okay," John said. "I didn't realize what I was saying was so ... wrong. I never would've said it, Maddie. Believe it or not, I'd never want to hurt you. I knew you growing up, and I was always fond of you. My brother is crazy about you, though, and I would never hurt you simply because it shreds him."

"I'm sorry for walking out," Maddie said. "It was immature. I don't know why I did it."

Christy glanced between her best friend and crush, conflicted. "What did he do to you?"

Nick reached over with his foot and nudged Christy. "Move to the other side of the booth."

"Maddie can sit here next to me," Christy said, patting the vinyl.

"I want her to sit with me," Nick said. "You can go to the other side of the booth with my brother and you two can feel each up under the table to your hearts' content."

Christy wrinkled her nose. "Good idea."

Once everyone was settled back at the table the waitress stopped by. "Can I continue your orders?"

"Yeah," Nick said. "I'm sorry about before. We'll make sure you get a big tip. Add the redhead's dinner to the bill and give it to my brother. He's buying."

The waitress beamed. "You've got it."

Conversation was light until their meals arrived, and then things turned serious.

"I'm really sorry, Maddie," John said.

"I still want to know what you did," Christy said, sipping from a glass of wine. "Did you make fun of them for looking like Barbie and Ken?"

John snickered. "No. I ... ."

"He knows," Maddie said quietly.

Christy's eyes widened. "Oh. Did you tell him, Nick?"

"No," Nick growled. "I would never tell anyone."

"You know?" John was surprised. "I thought no one knew but you, bro?"

"I figured it out on my own," Christy said.

"How?"

"I caught her talking to a ghost up at the kissing spot one night," Christy said. "Things just kind of fell into place."

"You can talk to ghosts, too?" John's eyes were wide. "No way."

"Oh, no," Christy said, wringing her hands. "I thought you said he knew."

"I knew about her being psychic," John said.

"Keep your voice down," Nick warned, glancing around to see if anyone was listening. "We don't need to tell the whole town."

"I'm sorry," John said. "This is crazy, though. How long have you known you could ... do that?"

"Since I was little," Maddie said, shifting uncomfortably next to Nick. He slung an arm over her shoulders to steady her. "I saw the first one when I was five. I didn't realize what was happening until I had a talk with my mom."

"And she could do that, too?"

"It runs in our family."

"Holy crap! Does that mean Maude ... ?"

Maddie immediately started shaking her head. "Granny doesn't have the peculiarity. It skips some generations."

"Do you wish it skipped you?" John was mesmerized with the conversation.

"Sometimes."

"I think it's cool," Christy said. "I've been trying to convince her to hold a séance so we can talk to some famous people. She won't do it."

"Leave her alone," Nick said. "That's just ... do you think we could talk to James Dean? I always thought he was cool."

Maddie rolled her eyes. "No. I wouldn't even know where to start with something like that. I don't seek them out. I usually just stumble across them."

"What about Hayley Walker?" Christy asked. "Have you been able to find her?"

"Not yet," Maddie said. "I was looking for her this afternoon, but I'm not sure she would be hanging around the pier if that's not where she died. I got distracted once I ran into Mildred, though. I think I'm going to try again tomorrow."

"Are you sure that's a good idea?" Nick asked.

"I'm sure that we need to find out who killed her," Maddie said. "Don't worry, I won't be out after dark and it's a pretty open area. I'll be perfectly safe."

"We'll talk about it at home tonight," Nick said.

"Speaking of that, I have no problem staying at your house again," Maddie said. "We need to check in on Granny tomorrow morning, though. I don't like thinking of her being on her own for two straight days when she's plotting against Harriet."

Christy snorted. "Harriet is probably dead and buried in the woods behind your house."

"Don't joke about that," Nick said, wagging his finger. "I don't need Maude getting any ideas."

"When does the construction start on her apartment?" Christy asked.

"The day after tomorrow," Maddie said. "I'm not looking forward to the mess, but I am happy she's getting what she wants. She's very excited to pick colors. She wants you and I to help her next week, by the way."

"Ooh, that sounds fun," Christy said. "I love interior decorating. After the construction is finished, are you going to finally move into your mother's bedroom?"

Nick tried to kick Christy under the table and missed, instead making contact with his brother's shin.

"Ow!" John glared at him. "Why did you do that?"

"What did you do?" Maddie asked, curious.

"Nothing," Nick said.

"He kicked me," John said. "I think he was aiming for Christy, though."

"Why?"

"He wants you to move into your mother's bedroom so there's enough room for him to move in there with you," John said. "Don't look at me that way, Nick. You need to tell her what you want."

"Why didn't you tell me?" Maddie asked.

"I've tried to talk to you about moving into the big room," Nick said, choosing his words carefully. "I know you don't want to displace your mom, so I'm letting it go."

"Olivia is dead, though," John said. "What? She is."

"It's probably harder for Maddie to take the room over because Olivia is still around," Christy said. "That's got to be hard."

"Wait, your mom is a ... ghost?"

Nick shot him a look. "I'm going to beat you. You just keep sticking your foot in your mouth at every turn."

"I didn't say it was a bad thing," John said. "I just ... it's amazing."

"It is amazing," Nick said. "It also makes things difficult for Maddie. It's not a big deal."

"Now ... wait a second," Maddie said. "Do you really want to move in with me once Granny is settled in her apartment? I'm not sure if she'll like that."

"She's the one who brought it up," Nick said.

"Oh. Wow."

"Mad, don't worry about it," Nick said. "We don't have to do anything right away. We've got time."

"Not if I'm buying your house," John said.

"You're selling your house?" Maddie's eyebrows shot up her forehead. "How come you didn't tell me any of this?"

"I haven't had time," Nick said. "We were ... busy ... last night and I didn't realize my brother was going to tell you everything I *secretly* confided in him. I thought I would be able to approach it in a sane way."

"You were busy last night?" Christy's face brightened. "Finally. I can't believe you didn't call me and give me all the dirty details this morning. I'm hurt."

"They were in bed until noon," John said. "The only reason they got up is because I made them."

"You're a bad brother," Christy said.

"I'm a good cop, though," John said. "As much as I want to continue to dig Nick's hole deeper, I think we need to talk about the case a few minutes."

"I hate you," Nick grumbled.

"I'm going to let you two go early tonight," John said. "I'm going to try and track down that Michael Jarvis kid and question him. He's probably not a suspect, but it's one thing to cross off our list for tomorrow."

"Michael Jarvis?" Christy wrinkled her nose. "Why are you questioning him?"

"Apparently he was hanging around with Hayley on the pier," Maddie replied.

"You guys know he's gay, right?"

"So we've been told."

"I can take you to the Jarvis house, John," Christy offered. "I know where it is, and that way you won't have to waste too much of your time."

"That sounds great."

Nick cleared his throat. "Didn't we talk about this earlier?"

"I can't remember," John said, feigning ignorance.

"Talk about what?" Christy asked.

"It doesn't matter," Nick said. "I just ... why don't we hold off questioning the Jarvis kid until tomorrow?"

"I've got it," John said. "Take your woman home and ... well, I'm guessing you two are going to have a big talk. Ha, ha."

"I really hate you," Nick said.

Maddie patted his knee under the table. "Don't worry. We're not just going to talk."

Nick smiled.

"We are going to talk first, though."

"Great," Nick said. "That's exactly how I saw us spending our time together tonight."


"WHAT are you doing out here, Mad?" Nick asked, sliding the glass door open and joining her on the deck. "I thought you wanted to yell at me."

"I don't want to yell at you, Nicky," Maddie said, leaning forward on the lawn chair so he could situate himself behind her. "I just want to know what you're thinking."

"I'm thinking I don't want to be away from you," Nick said. "I'm thinking I want us to share our lives."

"I thought that's what we were doing."

"We are," Nick said. "I still want to climb into bed next to you every night."

"We've been doing that."

"When I say 'I'm going home,' I want that to be a place you and I share."

Maddie sighed. "You could have just told me that. You didn't need to hide it."

"I was afraid I was moving too fast."

"We've only been together two weeks," Maddie said. "In our hearts, though, we've been together forever. It doesn't feel too fast."

"So, what's the problem?"

"There is no problem," Maddie said. "I've already talked to Bill Schroeder about sprucing up Mom's room when he's done with Granny's apartment. He's going to paint the walls and upgrade the shower in the bathroom. He's also going to refinish the wood floors throughout the entire house."

"Why didn't you tell me?"

"Because I was going to surprise you with a grand gesture," Maddie said.

Nick's heart rolled. "Oh. I'm guessing I ruined that for you."

"You could never ruin anything for me," Maddie said. "You've given me everything I've ever wanted. The truth is, I was worried about approaching you because I wasn't sure you'd want to give up this place. I know you love it here. It's just ... ."

"You love your house," Nick finished. "I know that. Olivia is there. Maude still has a few good years ahead of her. Who knows? She may never die. Your store is in that house. I picture our future in that house, Mad. Don't worry about that."

"But what about this place? You love it."

"I love you, Maddie," Nick said, kissing her neck. "You're my home. I'm not going to lie about missing this place, but that's why I'm selling it to my brother. It's going to stay in the family and I'm going to be able to come out here and fish whenever I want. This place isn't my home, though. I can't have a home that doesn't include you."

"Are you sure?"

"I've never been more sure of anything in my entire life," Nick said. "Besides, love, this house has two bedrooms. It's not big enough for when we decide to start a family."

Maddie balked. "You think about things like that?"

"I constantly think about our life," Nick said. "I think about it all."

"You don't want to have kids right away, do you? I was kind of hoping we'd have some time for just the two of us before we even consider that."

"We've got a lot of time," Nick said. "I don't want anything but you right now. I'd like a few years where we can be together without having any obligations. We could travel. We can go camping. We can take off in the middle of the night and go skinny-dipping." He poked her in the ribs, causing her to giggle. "I want kids with you some day. That day isn't right now, though."

"I love you, Nicky. I can't wait to move in with you."

"Me either," Nick said, kissing her softly. "Just because we don't want kids right away, though, that doesn't mean we can't practice."

"I'm glad you brought that up," Maddie said, beaming. "I have plans for you tonight."

"You mentioned that."

Maddie grabbed the sides of his face and held him steady. "Let's start now."

The kiss was deep and heartfelt, and unlike the night before, there were no nerves holding them back. Love is a funny thing, Nick mused. Just when you think you've felt all you can, someone comes along and makes you feel even more. Both Maddie and Nick were quickly realizing that there would never be a limit to their love, and they couldn't wait to see how far they could push the boundaries on their ongoing adventure. Tonight was just another step – and it was going to be a fun one.

## 14. FOURTEEN

"You didn't have to come with me," Maddie said, inserting her key into the lock and pushing the door of Magicks open. "I know you have work to do."

Nick nuzzled the side of her face as he moved up behind her, hormones from last night still raging. "I didn't want to be away from you yet."

"Nicky, you're acting like an addict," Maddie chided, although she was basking in the attention.

"I've been addicted to you my whole life," Nick said. "I just didn't realize how bad it was going to get when we started doing ... that."

"If you can't say the word out loud then you probably shouldn't be doing it," Maude said, breezing past the open door frame that led to the bowels of the house.

Nick grinned. "It looks like she's still alive. You were worrying for nothing."

"Just wait," Maddie said.

When they got to the kitchen they found ... chaos. Maude had set up four different dry erase boards on easels, and there were so many charts, graphs, and maps drawn on them Maddie was having trouble absorbing what she was seeing. "I ... what is this?"

"It's my plan for world domination," Maude said, shoving two mugs of coffee across the kitchen counter. "I'm glad you two finally surfaced. I need to talk to you."

"Is something wrong?" Maddie asked, worried. "Is it your hip? Did you fall? Is something wrong with the construction project?"

"Chill out, Nervous Nellie," Maude said, rolling her eyes. "I just wanted to tell you that I'm running for president of the Pink Ladies."

Nick pursed his lips to keep from laughing while Maddie tamped down her irritation. "Don't scare me like that again," Maddie instructed. "While I'm happy you're ... broadening your horizons ... that is not an emergency."

"When you're my age everything is an emergency," Maude said. "Grow up."

Nick snickered. "I see you're in good hands here, love." He kissed the back of her neck. "I need to find John and get moving."

"Where are you going to be today?"

"We're going up to the high school. They have a summer drama program, and we're hoping some of the kids will know about Hayley. It will be easier than tracking them all down separately. That's the one thing that blows about summer."

"Okay," Maddie said, kissing him lightly. "Call me if you come up with something."

"Where are you going to be?"

"Probably here," Maddie said.

"I thought you said you were going to go back down to the beach looking for Hayley's ghost?"

"I changed my mind, at least for now," Maddie said. "Until we know where Hayley died, looking for her ghost is going to be ... difficult. We don't even know if her ghost is still hanging around. I don't want to waste time there when I have stuff to do here."

"What stuff?"

"You're awfully suspicious this morning."

"I love you," Nick said. "What stuff?"

"You're very bossy," Maude said.

"I love you, too," Nick said. "Go back to your world domination plans."

"I'm going to open the store," Maddie said. "I didn't open yesterday because ... well ... you know."

"Everyone in town knows," Maude said. "They're accusing me of having inside information because I won the pool."

"A month ago that would've bugged me," Maddie said. "It doesn't bother me now. We're happy. Live with it."

Nick arched an eyebrow. "A month ago?"

"Fine. Two days ago. I'm trying to grow. Do you have to give me a hard time?"

Nick grinned. "I really do love you." He snagged a belt loop on her jeans and pulled her closer. "I'll call you later."

"I was hoping we could spend the night here tonight," Maddie said. "I ... um ... kind of want to show you the plans for Mom's bedroom. I thought we could pick colors out together."

Nick's heart jumped. "That sounds like a perfect evening. When I have more of a timetable I'll call you. I can bring dinner for all of us."

"Don't plan on feeding me," Maude said. "I have a strategy meeting with the women on my election team."

"I'm almost afraid to ask," Nick said. "What are you guys going to be doing?"

"Mostly drinking," Maude admitted. "Don't worry. I won't drive drunk. I'll spend the night over at Bernadette's house."

"Bernadette Dawkins?"

"Yes."

"Okay," Nick said. "Be good. Try not to get arrested."

"I'm always good," Maude said.

"Be better than that," Nick said. He gave Maddie one more kiss. "You be good, too."

"I'm always good," Maddie said.

"You're my angel," Nick agreed. "Maude, you should take some lessons from your granddaughter."

"You two are so sickly in love it makes me want to puke," Maude said.

"You'll live," Nick said. "You're going to have to. I'm moving in here once your apartment is done."

"I already knew that," Maude replied, nonplussed. "I knew that before you and Maddie did."

"You're very wise."

"I am," Maude agreed. "Don't worry. I'm fine with it. I like the idea of love filling this house again. It's felt lonely for far too long."

Nick's face softened. "There will be plenty of love here. You still have to behave yourself, though."

"You're such a killjoy."

**HOW** well do you know these kids?" John asked, parking in front of the high school and studying the teenagers milling on the lawn. "What do you think they're doing?"

"I know some of them," Nick said, studying the faces. "These are mostly the good kids. Trust me. The kids who are volunteering for a summer drama class – and it looks like they're painting sets over there – are not the kids getting drunk and rowdy up at Kissing Point."

John snickered. "I loved Kissing Point. I ruled there my senior year. You're probably jealous of that, aren't you?"

"Why would I be jealous of that?"

"Because you were sitting in fields staring at the sky and making wishes on stars with Maddie without the promise of any tongue action," John replied.

"How do you know that?"

"I told you already. I used to spy on you."

"Speaking of tongue action, what happened with you and Christy last night?"

John shifted in his seat. "Are you asking if I got lucky?"

"You better not have gotten lucky," Nick said. "Christy is a good woman. She doesn't deserve a broken heart."

"What makes you think I would break her heart?"

"Listen, I like Christy," Nick said. "I also think, one day, you're going to make someone a great husband. I don't think you're ready to settle down, though, and I do think Christy is looking for someone to share her life with."

"I could be ready to settle down," John argued.

"What makes you say that?"

"I see you with Maddie," John said. "The way you look at her is right out of a book. Right now I think it's out of one of those bodice rippers you see in the checkout line at the grocery store, but I also think it's right out of one of those big, sweeping romance stories. It makes me want what you have."

The admission warmed Nick. "You just can't decide to get that," he said. "It's something that happens. It's not something you can make happen."

"I know," John said. "I just ... I like Christy."

"Do you want to hurt her?"

"No."

"Then think really hard about this before you do anything," Nick said. "That's all I ask. Technically, you don't even live in this town yet and you're not going to for ... what ... two months? Can't you just wait until you're living here full time and you can really get to know Christy?"

"That's probably a good idea," John conceded.

"I only have good ideas." Nick pushed open his door and hopped out. "Now, come on. Let's see if we can solve a murder."

"One thing," John said, causing Nick to lean in and stare at his brother. "Did you and Maddie talk about everything last night?"

"We're picking colors for our new bedroom tonight," Nick said. "We're ... perfect."

"And you're back to being sloppy in love," John said. "I'm glad you're so predictable these days."

"Me, too."

"I'm also glad you're happy."

"Me, too."

**THE** students were leery to be approached by two police officers. Nick couldn't blame them. These were the types of kids unfamiliar with police questioning. That's why he liked them.

"We're not here accusing anyone of anything," Nick said. "I want to make that clear. We just need some help, and we knew you guys were up here today."

"What do you want to know?" Lexie Baker asked. "Are you here asking questions about Hayley Walker?"

"What do you know about that?" John asked.

"Just what everyone is saying," Lexie said. "They said she was found dead on the beach."

Justin Torkelson peered around Lexie's shoulder, his glasses slipping low on his nose. "They say she was naked and stabbed to death. Is that true?"

"No," Nick said. "She was fully clothed, and we're not saying how she died. I can say she wasn't stabbed, though. The coroner couldn't ascertain if she was raped or not."

"That means the rumors were true," Lexie mused.

"What do you mean?"

"If the coroner doesn't know if she was sexually assaulted that means she wasn't a virgin," Lexie said. "If she was still a virgin, you would've ruled sexual assault out."

Nick's mouth dropped open. "I ... ."

"Oh, don't be so surprised," Lexie said. "I'm going to school to be a medical examiner when I get out of this place. I watch a lot of television. I know things."

"Obviously," John said, shooting her a charming grin. "You're very smart."

"I'm also a lesbian," Lexie said. "That smile doesn't work on me. I don't like it."

"I like it," Justin said.

John shifted uncomfortably. "I ... ."

"You're not so smooth now, are you?" Nick asked.

"Shut up."

"Tell me about Hayley," Nick said. "Who were her friends?"

"She didn't have a lot of female friends," Lexie said. "She didn't get along with other girls."

"Why?"

"Because she was so slutty," Justin said.

Nick and John exchanged a look.

"Okay, here's how it works," Justin said. "Girls like each other in high school as long as everyone is exactly the same. When things start changing, that's when problems arise. Some girls become popular because they sleep around. When that happens, the other girls turn on them. To get popular, though, you have to sleep around. It's a vicious circle."

"It sounds like it," Nick said.

"Things were the same when we were in high school," John said. "You probably don't know that because you were wishing on stars with Maddie instead of doing the things you were supposed to be doing."

"I thought Maude won the pool," Justin said. "Is that not true?"

Nick shot him a look. "You know about the pool?"

Justin rolled his eyes. "If you'd moved a week faster I would've won. I'm still upset."

"Great," Nick said. "Tell me about Hayley's ... boyfriends."

"I don't know if I would call them boyfriends," Lexie said. "She spent a lot of time with Michael Jarvis, but he's ... ."

"Dating in a different pool," Justin supplied.

"I know," John said. "I talked to him last night. He seemed upset, but he didn't have any information for me."

"He probably just didn't want to talk badly about Hayley because he feels guilty," Lexie said.

"Why would he feel guilty?"

"He was trying to talk her out of dating Trevor Gardner. Hayley really liked him, though, and I think Michael and Hayley were fighting about it."

Nick racked his brain. "Trevor Gardner? Isn't he the big basketball star?"

"Yes," Lexie said. "He's very popular, and a lot of the girls want him. To get him, though, you had to be ... ."

"Adventurous," Nick said. "I get it."

"I was going to say slutty."

"Don't," Nick said. "That's not nice to say about someone."

"Don't worry, no one thinks your girlfriend is slutty," Lexie said. "Well, Marla Proctor does. Since Marla is slutty, her word doesn't hold much weight, though."

"This is the problem with living in a small town," Nick grumbled.

"Were Trevor and Hayley together at the time of her death?" John asked.

Lexie shrugged. "You'll have to ask him. Keeping up with Trevor's dating habits isn't part of my summer curriculum. Speaking of which, we need to get back to work."

Once it was just the two of them, Nick and John bent their heads together.

"What do you think?" John asked.

"I think we need to find Trevor Gardner. The prime suspect is always the boyfriend."

## 15. FIFTEEN

"Did you get any customers today?" Maude poked her head into Magicks and found Maddie sitting on the window seat.

"Yeah, I did pretty well," Maddie said. "I sold quite a few candles and gave two readings. It was good. I'm thinking that it might make sense to only be open a couple of days a week. People still come, and then it opens up my time."

"For Nick?" Maude teased, shuffling into the room.

"What would you think if I told you I was considering offering my help on some of Nick's cases?"

Maude smiled. "I think that would make you a very wonderful girl. You don't need my permission, though."

"I know," Maddie said. "It's just ... I wasn't sure I wanted to get involved in this stuff again. It's great when you have a missing person and you find them alive. When people die, though, it gets rough."

"I'm sure it does," Maude said. "You can't control that. You need to take the wins and let go of the losses. You can't save everyone, Maddie girl. That's the one thing that worries me about you. You desperately want to save everyone."

"It's taken me some time, but I think I can accept the losses now,"

Maddie said. "I like working with Nick, and I like knowing I'm helping people."

"Have you talked to Nick about this yet?"

"No," Maddie said. "He's the one who asked me to work with him on this case, though. I don't think he'll be opposed to it."

"I don't think so either," Maude said. "I do think he's going to put up a fight if you're constantly upset by people dying, though. He can't stand it when you're sad."

"I can't stand it when I'm sad either," Maddie said. "I just ... I think there's a way for me to keep Mom's legacy alive here and do good elsewhere. It's what I want to do."

"Then you can do it," Maude said. "You should know, though, that if you're going to be running around solving crimes with Nick people are going to be talking about your abilities even more than they do now."

"I used to think that was the worst thing in the world," Maddie admitted. "Then, last night, John just blurted out that he knew I was psychic."

"How did that go?"

"At first I jumped to the worst conclusion ever," Maddie said. "I thought Nick told him."

"He would never do that."

"I know," Maddie said. "I just ... I'm not used to someone always having my back."

"He's always had your back," Maude said. "He always will."

"Anyway, John was fine with it," Maddie said. "He figured it out on his own. In fact, he was kind of excited. It was just like when Christy found out."

"Well, I wouldn't go around bragging about it, but I'm certainly glad you're getting more comfortable in your own skin," Maude said. "You're practically glowing."

"I feel ... good."

"That makes me very happy," Maude said. "Now, I need to go and plot Harriet's bloody downfall. I won't be back tonight, so you and Nick can do ... whatever it is you want to do."

Maddie frowned. "I'm happier when you don't talk about it."

"You'll live," Maude said, patting her shoulder. "You'll get used to it. You're growing."

Maddie couldn't help but wonder if she really wanted to grow enough to feel comfortable talking about sex with her grandmother. Something told her she would draw the line there.

**TWO HOURS** later Maddie moved to the front door of Magicks to flip the sign and lock the door. Nick had texted that he was on his way, and instead of bringing dinner they were going to order pizza and snuggle together in the window seat to pick colors. To her, that sounded like a perfect evening.

To Maddie's surprise, the door opened at the exact second she was reaching for the doorknob. The teenage boy standing in the doorframe was exceedingly tall and excessively nervous. His hands were clenched in front of him, and he looked like he was about to pass out.

"Can I help you?" Maddie asked.

"I ... are you Maddie Graves?"

Maddie nodded.

"Good," the boy said, stepping inside and shutting the door behind him. "I need some help."

"Do you need a gift for someone?"

"I don't need that kind of help," the boy said. "I need your ... magical powers."

Maddie froze. "What?"

"You're psychic, right? That's what everyone in town says."

"Who are you?"

"Shouldn't you already know?" The boy ran a hand through his short-cropped brown hair. "I think a psychic should know something like that."

"That's not how it usually works," Maddie said. "Tell me your name."

"I'm Trevor Gardner. I'm going to be a senior at Blackstone Bay High School this year."

"Okay," Maddie said, gesturing toward one of the chairs in front of the big bay window. "Why don't you have a seat and tell me what's going on."

Once settled, Trevor fixed Maddie with a wan look. "I'm not sure where to start."

"I find the beginning is always best," Maddie prodded. "What's wrong?"

"They just found my girlfriend dead on the beach a few days ago," Trevor said. "If the town gossip is to be believed, you're the one who found her."

Maddie's heart skipped a beat. "I see. How long were you and Hayley dating?"

"Just a few weeks," Trevor said. "At first I wasn't even sure I wanted to date her. After talking to her, though, I realized she was pretty cool."

"That's good," Maddie said. "You must have been upset when she died. When was the last time you saw her?"

"Two days before her body was found," Trevor said. "I ... I'd been helping her hide."

Maddie leaned forward, surprised. "Hide from what?"

Trevor jumped up and started pacing, alternating between running his hands through his hair and wringing them together with enough force Maddie was worried he was going to cut off his own circulation.

"You need to calm down, Trevor," Maddie said.

"I can't. The cops came to my house today. They know I was dating Hayley."

"Where were you?"

"Up at the park shooting hoops," Trevor said. "My mom called the second they left. She wants to know what kind of trouble I'm in. The thing is, I'm not sure if I am in trouble. I was just trying to help Hayley. I still don't understand how she got from the cabin to the beach. It doesn't make any sense. She said she was staying in all night and I couldn't see her the next day because I had a basketball camp. No one but me knew she was even staying there."

"You need to go back in the story," Maddie said. "Tell me how you were helping Hayley. Why did she need help?"

"It's her dad," Trevor said, throwing himself back into the chair dramatically. "He was ... hurting her."

Maddie's heart clenched. "How?"

"He beat her sometimes," Trevor said. "She had a lot of bruises on her arms. That's why she was always wearing hoodies when it was hot. She didn't want people to know."

"Did he ... do anything else to her?" Maddie hated asking the question.

"I didn't ask," Trevor said, knowing what she was getting at. "She didn't want to talk about that ... stuff. I think so, though. She was really jumpy. Sometimes, when I tried to hug her, she was really stiff and uncomfortable."

"How did you help her?"

"My family has a hunting cabin on the far side of the lake," Trevor said. "We only use it a couple of weekends a year in the summer. It's really run down. We use it more in the fall when we go deer hunting, and the winter when we go ice fishing. We have a shanty right there. It works out."

"When did Hayley come to you and tell you all of this?"

"She told me after we'd been dating for about a week," Trevor said. "She had a horrible bruise on her ribs and I asked her what happened. She said her dad got drunk and threw her against a wall."

Maddie felt like throwing up. "Is that when you thought of the hunting cabin?"

Trevor nodded. "We made a plan," he said. "She went home one more night and packed some stuff up. She left a note for her mom and said that she was going to be staying with some friends. I took her out to the cabin that day, and she was happy to be there."

"How long was she there?"

"Two weeks."

"How often did you go out there?"

"As often as I could," Trevor said. "I told my parents I was playing basketball at the park, but I was really out at the cabin with Hayley."

"What was she doing?"

"Mostly reading. She loved books. She was also making a plan to go to the police. We knew she couldn't stay out there forever. She was hoping that, as soon as she got her courage up, she would be able to get her father arrested and return home. That was the plan anyway."

"Do you think she told anyone else her plans?"

"She was only close with me," Trevor said. "She and Michael were in a fight, so I know she wasn't talking to him."

"You're talking about Michael Jarvis, right?"

"Yeah. They were best friends until they started fighting about me. I felt bad for getting between them. I thought when things calmed down they would make up. I guess they never got the chance. It's hard when your best friend is a boy when you're a girl ... and vice versa, I guess."

Maddie knew the realities of that life. "It is," she said. "How was Hayley acting the last time you saw her?"

"She was nervous," Trevor said. "She was also ... ready. We were planning on going to the police department together the next day. I woke up to news of her death, though, and ... well ... I've just been trying to figure things out since. I don't know what to do. I thought you would be able to help."

"Why didn't you go to the police after you heard?"

"Honestly? I was worried my mom would flip out because I was hiding her," Trevor said. "My mom is really high strung. She's a good mom, don't get me wrong, but she overreacts to everything."

"I think that's a mom's job," Maddie said, sympathetic. "Have you been back out to the cabin?"

Trevor shook his head. "I couldn't bring myself to go out there. I don't know why. I just get this sense of ... dread ... when I think about it. I keep hoping this is all a dream and I'll wake up and she'll still be alive."

"I know that feeling, Trevor," Maddie said. "Life isn't a dream, though, and you need to tell the police what you know."

"What if they think I killed her?"

"I'm sure they're going to ask you some tough questions," Maddie said. "I'm also sure they're not going to jump to conclusions. They want to find out what really happened to Hayley. I think you owe her. Someone needs to pay for what they've done to her."

"Do you think it was her dad?"

"I don't know," Maddie said. "I do know you have answers to some really important questions, though. The good news for you is that Nick is on his way here now. I promise he'll listen to you."

"I guess I don't have a choice," Trevor said. "I ... do you think we can wait for him outside? I could use some air."

"I think that's fine," Maddie said, getting to her feet. "Come on. We can wait on the front porch. You can collect yourself. It's going to be okay."

"Hayley is gone," Trevor said. "That's never going to be okay."

Maddie followed Trevor out onto the porch, frowning when she saw Nick's truck already in the driveway. The driver's seat was empty, and Nick was nowhere in sight. "I ... where is Nick?"

"Maybe he ... oomph." Trevor tilted sideways as Nick barreled into him from the side, appearing out of nowhere. The teenager was caught so off guard he couldn't maintain his balance and tumbled to the hard wood below.

Nick was on top of him, and he was using his impressive muscle mass to hold the boy down as he struggled. "You're safe, Maddie. I've got him. I saved you. Everything is going to be okay."

Maddie wasn't so sure.

## 16. SIXTEEN

"Get off me."

"Stay down there."

"My shoulder hurts, man. Get off me."

"You'll live ... and you're lucky I didn't kill you for going after my girlfriend." Nick was beside himself as he shifted his body weight to keep Trevor pinned to the ground. "Are you okay?"

Maddie was unsure how to proceed. Nick appeared to be a man on the edge and Trevor ... well ... he wasn't in any immediate danger. "Hi, Nicky," she said, purposely keeping her voice even. "How was your day?"

"Great," Nick said. "I found out this kid was dating Hayley Walker. When I went to his house he wasn't there. Instead, I found him here going after you. I'm just ... peachy."

"Um ... ."

"I wasn't going after your girlfriend," Trevor sputtered. "I was trying to get her to help me."

"I don't believe you."

"Nicky, he's telling the truth," Maddie said, extending her hand and tentatively placing it on his shoulder. "He didn't threaten me. We were just talking."

Nick relaxed his stance, if only marginally. "What?"

"He just wanted some help," Maddie said. "He's upset. We were going onto the front porch to wait for you. He never raised a finger toward me."

"Oh," Nick said, pulling back slightly. "I thought he came here to hurt you."

"Why would I want to hurt her?" Trevor asked, tilting his head in an attempt to get a better look at Nick. "What possible reason would I have to hurt her?"

"You'd be surprised," Nick said, pushing himself up from the ground and helping Trevor to his feet. "People have tried to kill her twice in the last six weeks. She's important to me. I don't want her hurt."

"Well ... I guess we have that in common," Trevor said, dusting his jeans off while shooting a dark look in Nick's direction. "You're kind of a spazz."

Nick scowled. "I am not a spazz." He looked to Maddie for help. "Tell him I'm not a spazz."

"You're very handsome," Maddie said, rubbing her thumb against his cheek to wipe a smudge of dirt. "I also love you very much."

"I am not a spazz," Nick grumbled, crossing his arms over his chest as he regarded Trevor. "What are you doing here?"

"I ... ." Trevor's bravado faded.

"He has a few things to tell you," Maddie said. "I told him you would be fair and hear him out. Of course, that was before you tackled him."

"Don't push it, Mad," Nick said. "I just about had a heart attack when I saw him with you. After what happened with Todd ... and the mayor ... you can't blame me for worrying about you."

"It's because you're smoking hot," Trevor said. "If you were my girlfriend I'd tackle anyone that looked at you, too."

"Thanks," Nick said, running his hand through his hair. "I think."

"He was complimenting me," Maddie said.

"I snagged you," Nick countered. "He was complimenting me."

Maddie rolled her eyes. "Do you want to sit down?"

"Do I need to sit down?"

Maddie exchanged a look with Trevor. "Actually, no. I think we all need to take a drive. Trevor can tell you what he told me on the way. It will be dark soon, and I think it's better that we leave now."

"You want to take him out there tonight?" Trevor asked, dubious.

"Yes," Maddie said. "He's going to want to see it tonight, and this way we'll be cutting out all that middle stuff and we won't be wasting time."

"Where are we going?" Nick asked.

"It's a long story," Maddie said. "Trust me, though, you're going to want to hear it."

Nick studied her for a moment, taking in the serious tilt of her head and somber eyes, and then he turned to Trevor. "You're riding in the passenger seat. It's not that I don't trust you but ... ."

"She's smoking hot," Trevor said. "I get it."

Maddie grinned at Nick as Trevor started moving toward his Explorer. "Did you hear that? I'm smoking hot."

"I already knew that," Nick said, leaning down to give her a kiss. "You scared me, Mad. I'm sorry if I embarrassed you."

"I'll forgive you this time," Maddie said. "Knowing you did it out of a place of love helps."

"Move your cute little butt," Nick said. "I want to know what he's doing here, and I want to hear it all and still have time to spend with you tonight. I've been fantasizing about you all day."

"I'm sure we can figure something out."

"WHY didn't you come straight to us?" Nick asked, frustrated as he glanced around the hunting cabin.

The structure – more of a shack really – consisted of one main room with a tiny kitchenette in the corner and a bathroom off to the left side. There was a set of bunk beds pushed against one wall, and a handful of clothes were strewn about on the floor near the bed. In addition to the clothes, a multitude of other items were tossed around haphazardly – almost as if someone had been going through Hayley's things looking for something specific.

"Hayley was afraid," Trevor said. "She wouldn't stop crying. She needed time to ... come to grips with stuff. I honestly thought I was helping."

"You were," Maddie said, fixing Nick with a quelling look. "You did the best you could. You were trying to save her. You were trying to ... protect her. I'm sure Nick understands that feeling."

Nick rolled his eyes. "We're not talking about you and me right now. We could have helped them. We would have made sure that she was safe."

"Would you have done any differently if it was me?"

Nick frowned. "Probably not. You be quiet for a few minutes, though. You can yell at me later." He turned back to Trevor. "Did the cabin look like this the last time you were up here?"

"No. Hayley liked things clean. In fact, when I was up here, she spent half of her time cleaning up after me."

"Do you think anyone could've followed you up here?"

"No."

"Think hard, Trevor," Nick said. "Did anyone know she was up here?"

"I don't see how," Trevor said. "I was really careful. I kept expecting her father to bust through the door of my house looking for her ... but it never happened."

"I just don't know what to think," Nick said. "I talked to her parents the day after we found her body. They were ... upset."

"Maybe they were upset because they killed her," Maddie suggested.

"Maybe," Nick said, searching his memory. "The father seemed really ... quiet. Stoic. He didn't cry, but that's not unusual. Sometimes it takes a few hours ... days even ... for something like that to sink in."

"What about her mother?"

"She cried," Nick said. "She worked really hard to contain herself and not fall apart, but there were tears."

Maddie glanced at Trevor. "What do you know about her mother?"

"Not much," Trevor said. "She hated her father ... I mean really hated him. She never talked much about her mother. I thought that was weird. I just assumed her father was beating her mother, too."

"I would guess he probably is," Nick said. "That might explain why she was so muted when we told her about Hayley's death. She's probably used to swallowing her feelings."

"What are you going to do?" Maddie asked.

"I'm going to talk to John, and then I guess we're going to question the parents again tomorrow," Nick replied. "I'm also going to get a tech team up here to run prints and process the scene."

"Scene?" Trevor's face drained of color. "Do you think she was killed up here?"

"I don't know," Nick said honestly. "I think it looks like there might have been a struggle. That lamp was knocked off the table, and someone clearly went through all of Hayley's things."

"Do you think they were looking for something?" Maddie asked.

"That would be my guess," Nick said. "Did Hayley have anything of value? Jewelry? Money?"

"No."

"Well, I guess we just have to take this one step at a time," Nick said. "The first step is talking to your parents."

Trevor shifted uncomfortably. "Is that absolutely necessary?"

"This is their property," Nick said. "You're a minor. You can't give consent for a search. Call them."

"But ... ."

"Call them or I will," Nick said. "It's going to be better coming from you. Trust me."

"What if they yell?"

"They're your parents," Nick said. "They're probably going to be upset at first ... but they're going to understand. Call them."

"I'm going to walk around outside," Maddie said, keeping her voice low.

Nick glanced at her. "Mad ... ."

"I just want to see if she's here," Maddie said. "If this is where she died ... ."

"Love, I don't want you wandering around outside alone," Nick said. "If Hayley did die here, that means a murderer could be hanging around and watching this place."

"I won't go far," Maddie said. "I promise. I have to know, though."

Nick growled. "You keep your phone in your pocket and you stay within shouting distance of this cabin. I'm not joking, Mad. I have to stay in here with Trevor. If you see anything ... if you sense anything ... if your hair even stands on end ... I want you to yell for me. I will come running."

"It's going to be okay, Nicky."

"I just got you, Maddie. I don't want to lose you. Not ever."

"I promise to be careful," Maddie said. "I just need to see."

Nick leaned over and gave her a sweet kiss. "Stay close."

"Always."

**TRUE TO** her word, Maddie remained close enough to the cabin to touch it as she circled. She kept one ear to her surroundings, and the other to her inner senses. If Hayley's ghost was here, she would feel it.

After walking around the cabin twice – it was a short trip – Maddie found frustration to be her new walking mate. In her head she knew the odds of Hayley's ghost making an appearance were small. In her heart, though, she couldn't help but yearn for it. She wanted to help. She wanted to make sure a tortured teenager found solace and relief in death. That didn't look to be happening this evening.

Impulsively Maddie reached out and pressed her fingertips against the roughened wood walls of the cabin. The second she made contact her world tilted, and she flashed into someone else's nightmare.

Maddie pressed her eyes shut, giving in to the vision. While she usually got visions when she was at her most relaxed – in sleep – on occasion she had been privy to a waking vision. They were almost always powerful ... and disturbing.

Maddie's mind was foggy, and she leaned her forehead against the cabin to steady herself. She could hear raised voices, and even though the vision didn't clear, Maddie opened her mind's ear and listened.

*"I don't care what you say. I'm going to do what I have to do. You might not want it, but it's what's going to happen. I know what's right and wrong, and I'm not going to pretend that what's going on isn't wrong. I want a life."*

The unmistakable sound of skin smacking against skin assailed Maddie's ears. Someone had struck someone, but no matter how hard she concentrated Maddie couldn't clear up the vision. It was just voices ... and an overwhelming sense of terror.

*"Don't you touch me! Not again! I won't stand for it."*

This time no one struck anyone. Instead, Maddie could feel the cold hands of death closing around her throat. She opened her mouth to yell for Nick, even though she knew there was nothing he could do to stop the vision. This wasn't happening – not to her, at least – and yet she couldn't separate herself from Hayley's memory.

It was too much.

Maddie's knees started to buckle, and just as she was about to hit the ground she felt a pair of strong arms catch her.

"Maddie."

*Nicky.* Maddie opened her mouth, but no sound came out.

"Talk to me, Maddie." Nick propped her body against his, panicked. "What's happening?"

When Maddie didn't answer, he shook her. Hard.

"Maddie!"

## 17. SEVENTEEN

"I can walk myself into the restaurant."

After finally catching her breath – and almost giving Nick a heart attack – Maddie regained her senses relatively quickly. Nick was glued to her side, even when Trevor's parents stormed into the cabin and proceeded to have a rather impressive meltdown. The only time Nick left Maddie was when the tech team arrived. He gave them specific instructions and then immediately returned to her. They hadn't talked about what she'd seen – Nick was giving her time to process – but instead of ordering pizza Nick was insistent on getting some food in her before returning to the house.

"Maddie, if I thought I could carry you into this restaurant without making a scene I would," Nick said.

"I'm okay."

"I'm not. You scared the life out of me."

"I'm ... sorry."

Nick stilled, pulling Maddie to him and hugging her tightly. "You don't need to apologize. I'm sorry. You just ... I thought you were going to stop breathing."

"I saw ... or more like felt ... Hayley's last moments. She did die in that cabin."

"Okay," Nick said, kissing Maddie's temple. "We don't have to talk about it here. I just want to get some food into you and get you into bed. You need to rest."

"Oh, we're still picking paint colors tonight," Maddie said. "I was looking forward to that all day."

"We'll see."

"I'm getting my way," Maddie said, pulling away from Nick and stalking toward the restaurant. "I absolutely refuse to let this ruin my night."

Nick scowled but followed her, almost running into her on the other side of the door because she'd abruptly stopped. "Did you change your mind? Are you going to let me carry you?" He was going for levity.

"I was wrong about something not ruining my night," Maddie said.

"What?"

She pointed, and Nick's heart sank when he saw the two women sitting at the round table in the center of the room. Cassidy and Marla had their heads bent together, and they were laughing about something so they hadn't seen Nick and Maddie yet.

"We can go back to the house if you want. I'll find something there to cook."

"No," Maddie said, shaking her head. "I'm done hiding. I want some soup and a grilled cheese, and I know very well you want a burger."

Nick smiled, enjoying her "take charge" attitude despite the worry plaguing him for the past hour. "I love you, Maddie."

"I love you, too. Now ... let's just sit down. I'm sick of having to tiptoe around the two of them. I'm just ... done."

"Now I really love you."

"We're looking at paint tonight, too."

"You're so bossy," Nick said, putting his hand to the small of Maddie's back and urging her toward their favorite corner booth. "I like you bossy."

. . .

"**DO YOU** two want your usual?" Ruby's Diner had been a favorite hangout for Nick and Maddie when they were teenagers. It was no surprise then that, as adults, they opted to go there at least once a week.

"Yeah, Ruby," Nick said. "My usual is great."

"I want some of your tomato macaroni soup and a grilled cheese on whole wheat," Maddie said, smiling at the aging proprietress.

Ruby arched an eyebrow. "Comfort food? Did you already tick her off, Nick?" Ruby studied them a moment, taking in the way they softly touched one another in the center of the circular booth. "It doesn't look like she's mad. What else is wrong? I have two months down the road for your first fight in the pool, so try to hold off."

Nick scowled. "Don't you guys have anything better to do than hold nonsensical pools?"

"Apparently not." Ruby leaned over and pushed a strand of Maddie's hair back so she could get a better look at her. "You're pale."

"She's not feeling well," Nick said. "I think she might be coming down with a cold."

"You're a bad liar," Ruby said, nonplussed. "Whatever it is, I'm sure she'll be fine. She's survived two killers in six weeks. She's made of sterner stuff than any of us thought."

"I always knew she was made of stern stuff," Nick said, poking Maddie in the ribs. "I like her ... stern."

"You like her any way you can get her," Ruby said. "By the way, you should be aware that the Devil and her minion at the middle table have been talking about you two nonstop since you came in."

"We saw them," Nick said. "We're opting to ignore them."

"That's probably smart," Ruby said. "I'm just not sure that Marla is going to ignore you. I don't think she's made that way."

"We'll be okay," Maddie said. "They can't hurt us."

"Oh, you two are so stinking cute," Ruby said, rolling her eyes when Nick kissed Maddie's cheek. "You make me want to smack you both."

"I thought you always knew we were going to end up together?" Nick challenged. "That's what you told me."

"That doesn't mean you're not gross," Ruby said. "At least you're adorable while you're doing it."

"Thank you," Maddie said.

"I'll put a rush on your food," Ruby said. "Maddie looks like she's going to keel over."

"She's eating her dinner and then going straight to bed," Nick said.

"I've heard you two have been doing that a lot lately," Ruby teased.

"Ha, ha."

"I'll be back," Ruby said. "Just keep an eye on the devils."

Once Ruby was gone Nick used the moment of quiet to study Maddie's face. "Are you really okay?"

"I'm fine," Maddie said. "I don't usually get visions when I'm awake. When I do, they're ... harder to stomach."

"What happened?"

"I thought you wanted to wait until we got home?"

"Now I have other things I want to do when we get home," Nick said, grinning.

"Picking paint better be one of those things."

"It is," Nick said. "I just plan on having you naked when we do it."

Maddie wrinkled her nose and leaned in so she could kiss him. "Deal."

"Tell me what you saw."

"I didn't *see* anything," Maddie said. "I heard a girl yelling at someone and saying that she was going to do the right thing. Then I heard someone smack someone. Then ... well ... I felt someone being strangled."

Nick's eyes widened. "You were being strangled?"

"I felt what Hayley was going through. There's a difference."

"I saw your face, Maddie," Nick said. "You were feeling everything she felt." He pulled her closer. "I wish you didn't have to go through things like that."

"I know you do. We can't change it, though. We just have to take what we can get from the visions and go from there."

"You're being brave for me," Nick said. "I appreciate it. I still don't like it."

"It's going to be okay, Nicky."

"I know it is," Nick said. "You're going to eat and then I'm putting you in bed. It's going to be fine."

"Now you're being the bossy one."

"We'll share the onus of being bossy. It's a hard job. It's going to take two of us."

"Oh, you're so cute."

"You're cuter." Nick cupped the back of Maddie's head and kissed her softly.

"Good grief! Get a room."

The romantic moment was broken by the sound of Marla's nasally voice. When Nick turned to face her, he found Cassidy and Marla staring at them. The diner was tiny enough for everyone to hear Marla's comment. "We plan on getting a room as soon as we're done eating."

"Maybe you should have ordered in," Marla suggested. "That would have been the polite thing to do."

"Or you could just not look," Nick said. "That would also be the polite thing to do."

"Its hard to ignore the two of you when you're purposely flaunting your indiscretion in front of the woman whose heart you broke," Marla said.

"Oh, shut up, Marla," Nick said.

"Excuse me?"

"Get over it," Nick said. "We're together. We're happy. I'm sorry you two are so miserable you can't just ... suck it up ... but that's not our problem. It's your problem."

"You have no shame, do you?"

Nick opened his mouth to answer, but Maddie cut him off. "No, we don't. We don't have anything to be ashamed about."

"You're not ashamed of stealing another woman's man?" Marla challenged.

"Nope," Maddie said. "I'm proud of myself. I've gotten what I've always wanted. I'm not going to go out of my way to hide from you. Not any longer. I'm sorry you were hurt, Cassidy, but I can't keep apologizing."

"I guess that's easy for you to say since you're just starting your six-month cycle," Cassidy sneered. "Talk to me again when your six months are up and he dumps you."

"Hey." Nick leaned forward, angry. "Your problem is with me. Stop taking it out on Maddie. And, while we're at it, you knew very well when we started dating that I had a certain *reputation*. It's not my fault you thought you were going to somehow be the one to break the cycle.

"Everyone in this town knew there was only one person who was going to break it," he continued. "I knew it. I didn't want to admit it, but I knew it. Cripes, I never even introduced you to my family. That should have tipped you off that you had a limited shelf life."

Maddie patted his leg under the table, worried. "Calm down."

"I'm sorry," he said, leaning back and slipping his arm around Maddie's shoulders so he could center himself. "That was mean. It was the truth, though."

"Aren't you worried, Maddie?" Marla asked, ignoring Cassidy's crestfallen expression. "Aren't you worried he's going to get bored with you and dump you just like he did Cassidy? Come on. You can tell me. It has to be going through your mind. You're too insecure to ignore it."

Maddie sighed heavily. "I was a little worried about it at first," she said.

"Mad ... ."

Maddie cut Nick off with a brief look. "Then we decided to move in together." It was wrong. She knew that. She was taking a small amount of pleasure in the disgusted look on Marla's face and another small amount of pleasure from the hurt look on Cassidy's face. She couldn't help herself, though. She wanted people to know they were moving forward.

"You're moving in together?" Cassidy was horrified. "You've been dating for three weeks. You can't move in together."

"Well, we are," Nick said. "I'm selling my house to my brother and then I'm moving to Maddie's house with her."

"Our house," Maddie corrected.

Nick tightened his grip on Maddie's shoulder. "Our house."

"You're just doing this to spite me, aren't you?" Cassidy was near tears. "You want to prove a point. You want the whole town to think you dumped me because she's your true love. You don't want to be the bad guy, so this is how you're getting around it."

"Where you're concerned, I am the bad guy," Nick said. "I get it, and I don't expect to be treated otherwise. I treated you poorly. I am sick to death of you going after Maddie, though. She didn't do anything to you."

"And yet you're still going to move in with her just to spite me," Cassidy spat.

"I'm moving in with her because I love her and we're going to build a life together," Nick said. "This is our first step."

"It's pretty easy with Maude there as a buffer," Marla scoffed.

"Maude is converting the garage into a private apartment," Nick said. "In five weeks, she'll still be a part of our home and have her own personal space at the same time."

Cassidy's mouth dropped open, stunned. "You're displacing that poor old woman just to get to me?"

Maddie slammed her hands down on the table, taking Nick by surprise. "You're not a part of the equation, Cassidy," she said. "I don't know how many different ways we can tell you that. We're both sorry that you got hurt, but enough is enough."

Cassidy burst into tears, causing Marla to rub her back and shoot daggers in Maddie and Nick's direction. "Nice."

Ruby picked that moment to walk out of the kitchen carrying a takeout bag. She dropped it on the table in front of Maddie and Nick and smiled at them sympathetically. "I figured you'd want to take this to go."

"You figured right," Nick said, digging into his wallet. "I'm sorry for causing a scene."

"They caused the scene," Ruby said. "Don't worry about it. I'm going to have a little talk with Marla as soon as you go. If she can't abide by the rules I set up for her when she was a teenager, she doesn't need to come back."

"I heard that," Marla snapped.

"You were meant to," Ruby said. "Keep it up and you'll be banned from every business in town."

Nick dropped a few bills on the table and flashed a cheeky grin in Ruby's direction. "I've always loved you."

"Right back at you, handsome. Now take your real love and get her into bed. She's had a big night. She finally stood up to the resident devil and she's going to pick paint colors."

"You heard that?"

"I always keep my ears open for good news," Ruby said. "Have fun tonight. You two have earned it."

## 18. EIGHTEEN

"Well, I'm officially impressed," Nick said, pulling the covers back so he could slide underneath them and cuddle up next to Maddie. "You stood up for yourself."

"I stood up for us."

Nick smiled. "You did. How do you feel?"

"Guilty."

Nick's smile turned upside down. "Why?"

"Because I only told them we were moving in together to win," Maddie said. "For a second there I wanted to make them feel bad."

"I always want Marla to feel bad."

Maddie arched an eyebrow. "What about Cassidy?"

"I don't know what you want me to do about Cassidy," Nick said. "I feel bad for what I did, but I don't feel bad for being happy. I've apologized. I don't expect her to forgive me and let bygones be bygones. I'm still tired of putting up with that ... face."

"She's very pretty," Maddie said. "Her skin is ... gorgeous."

"That's not what I'm talking about," Nick said, poking Maddie's side. "She looks at me like I posted naked photos of her on the Internet and then dumped her the next day. She made things as hard as she possibly could. That's not my fault."

"I'm not saying it's your fault," Maddie said. "I'm saying I feel bad about purposely telling her we were moving in together because I wanted her to feel bad. No, don't say anything. I did. I didn't think it long, and once the words were out of my mouth I felt horrible, but I did say it to win."

"You've officially won, love," Nick said, rubbing his hand over her flat abdomen. "I'm the ultimate prize."

Maddie snorted. "You're lucky you're cute because your ego is just ... out of control."

"I'm willing to show you something else that's out of control," Nick said, pressing his lips to Maddie's jaw gently. "Or ... are you too tired?"

"I told you I'm fine," Maddie said. "It was a rough few minutes, but I wasn't really hurt."

"You looked hurt to me."

"I'm fine," Maddie said. "Besides, I have plans for you tonight."

"That's exactly what I wanted to hear." Nick eagerly yanked on his boxers as Maddie reached toward the nightstand on her side of the bed. When she fanned the paint wheel out Nick frowned, his boxers hovering over the side of the mattress. "What is that?"

Maddie feigned innocence. "It's a paint wheel. I thought we were going to pick paint colors."

*Paint colors? Crap.* Nick pursed his lips. "I forgot."

"We are moving in together," Maddie said. "Don't you think we should pick the color of our bedroom together?"

Picking paint colors wasn't high on Nick's to-do list, but he nodded his head anyway. She was intent on the paint colors. If they spent five minutes picking something out she would be happy ... and then he would be happy. "Sure," Nick said, tossing his boxers over the side of the bed and snuggling her close. "What color do you like?"

"I don't know," Maddie said. "I was thinking a nice blue would work. We don't want something too feminine."

Nick wouldn't have cared if the walls were covered with flowers and photos of little shoes. "Blue it is. See? That was easy." He ran his hand over Maddie's stomach again, pressing his lips to her cheek. "Come here."

"We have to pick a color first," Maddie reminded him, internally laughing at the frustrated look on his face.

"We just did. We picked blue."

Maddie fanned out the color wheel. "There are hundreds of different shades of blue."

"Are you trying to kill me?"

Maddie ignored him. "I like a lighter blue. If we go too dark it will make the room feel smaller."

"Maddie?"

"Hmm."

"How about you pick the blue? I'll like any blue you pick."

"But ... we're supposed to be doing this together."

Nick faltered. *Why was this so important to her?* "Mad, I don't care about the paint. I care about sharing a bedroom with you. Paint it black. I really don't care."

Maddie jutted her lower lip out. "Okay."

*Was she playing him?* "Fine. We can pick paint." Nick pulled his hand away and ran it through his hair. "Show me some blue."

Instead of lifting the paint wheel Maddie leaned over and rested her head on Nick's chest, batting her baby blue eyes up at him.

"What are you doing?"

"You told me to show you some blue."

This time Nick couldn't help but grin. "You're just screwing with me, aren't you?"

"Not yet."

Maddie tossed the paint wheel onto the nightstand. "I don't want to hear one complaint about the color."

"Make it the color of your eyes and you've got a deal," Nick said, wrapping his arm around her waist and tugging her the rest of the way on top of him. "That's my absolute favorite color in the world. It always has been."

"That is a vicious lie," Maddie said, laughing. "You told me that red was your favorite color when we were kids."

"I just didn't want your ego to get too big."

"Ah, well, that makes perfect sense." They kissed, their hearts sinking into the same excited rhythm.

"Did you lock the door?" Nick asked, reaching for the lamp beside the bed. "I know Maude said she wasn't coming home tonight, but I don't want to take any chances."

"I handled it, Nicky," Maddie said. "Now shut up and kiss me."

"Did I mention how much I love this new bossy side of you?"

"Yes. Now take your shirt off."

**MADDIE** was swimming in a sea of bliss, the warmth of Nick's body anchoring her to a shared moment of pure happiness. She could see herself gazing out at the water, recognizing she was on the lake because the beach was speeding by, but inherently she knew she was still in bed with Nick.

Why was she flying over the water when she was really sleeping with Nick? The reality hit her quickly. She wasn't flying. She was in a boat.

In her dreamlike state Maddie was caught between two worlds. Her heart was soaring, the feeling of Nick's love washing over her with each breath he expelled on her neck. Her head was trying to understand what she was looking at.

The boat wasn't big, probably about twenty-five feet from cabin to stern. Since the white edges were hazy, though, it was hard to ascertain what kind of boat she was on. In fact, Maddie couldn't remember the last time she was even on a boat. When she was younger she used to love it when Nick took her out for afternoon excursions on his father's boat. That was one thing they hadn't done together since she'd returned. She made a mental note to ask him about taking a boat ride, and then focused on the dark figure behind the wheel.

It wasn't a person – not the in the strictest sense of the word, that is. It was more of a shadow, a feeling. Everything emanating from it was malevolent. Given the lack of shape and form, Maddie couldn't ascertain if she was looking at a man or a woman. She just knew it was evil. Why was she even here?

"You're here because of me."

Maddie snapped her head to the side, surprised to see Hayley Walker standing next to her. Unlike the dark figure on her left, Hayley was surrounded by an aura of white light on her right. "Hayley. Why are you here?"

"I'm not here," Hayley said, hunkering down next to Maddie. "You're looking for me. I know that. I'm not here, though. I didn't ... hold on."

Maddie didn't know what to say. Nothing like this had ever happened to her before. "Did you cross over?"

"I crossed over right away," Hayley said. "I didn't want to stay."

"Why? Didn't you want justice?"

"There was no justice for me, not in the sense you mean anyway," Hayley said. "When I knew what was happening it was just easier to let go. This world has been nothing but ... hard ... for me. I was ready to go to a place that wasn't about constant pain."

"Did your father ... hurt ... you?"

"He never did anything else."

"Did he ... ?" Maddie wasn't sure how to ask the question. How do you ask a teenage girl if the man who helped give her life also sexually assaulted her?

"I don't like to think about it," Hayley said. "It's not important now. I am ... beyond this place."

"Then why are you here?"

"You called me here."

"I did?"

"Your soul did," Hayley said. "Your soul is searching for mine, even if you don't realize it. They touched this afternoon."

"I felt that," Maddie said, her eyes sad. "I'm sorry about what happened to you."

"I didn't die there," Hayley said.

"I felt you die."

"You felt me lose consciousness," Hayley countered. "That's not where I died. Why do you think we're here?"

Maddie considered the question. "No one saw anyone go to the cabin because they didn't approach from the road. That's it, isn't it? They approached in a boat."

"I would've heard someone approach from the road," Hayley explained. "I would've had time to run. I heard boats on the lake all the time. It never occurred to me that one would be stopping here."

"Do you know who came for you?"

"Darkness."

"I need more than that."

"I can't give it to you," Hayley said.

"Why not? Don't you want someone to pay for killing you?"

"I'm not really here," Hayley said. "You brought part of me to you, but it's not all of me. I can't give you the answers you want."

"What can you give me?"

"I can only tell you that you're close to discovering the truth of my death, but you may lose your own life in the search," Hayley said. "Be very careful, Maddie Graves. You live your life on the edge of two worlds, and I think one of them would love to claim you early."

Maddie swallowed hard. "Are you ... happier?"

"I couldn't be any sadder so ... yes ... I'm happier."

"Do you need me to tell anyone anything?"

"Tell Trevor I'm sorry and I should have listened to him," Hayley said. "He wanted me to go to the police right away. He was right."

"He's upset."

"I know," Hayley said. "I'm not worried about him, though. He'll be fine."

"Can you see his future?"

"I could see his future before I died," Hayley said. "He was always destined for greatness. This won't stop him."

"I'll tell him."

"I need you to tell Michael something, too."

"Michael Jarvis?"

"He's the best friend I've ever had," Hayley said. "We were fighting when ... he probably hates me."

"He's your best friend," Maddie said. "He'll always love you. That's the way of best friends."

"Probably," Hayley said. "I need you to tell him that he was wrong about Trevor, but he was right about me. I was searching for something, and just because he couldn't love me the way I wanted to be loved that doesn't mean he didn't love me better than anyone else in this world ... or the next."

Maddie choked up. "I ... ."

"I'm out of time," Hayley said. "You're about to wake up. Look at the boat. Look at me. Remember the boat. Remember me."

"I ... I can't see anything."

"Look harder."


"MADDIE!"

Nick shook Maddie gently, his heart rolling as she whimpered in her sleep. He pulled her flush against his chest, kissing her forehead as he tried to wake her without jolting her.

"Love, come on. Come back to me."

Maddie's eyes flew open and she burst into tears when she saw Nick's concerned face.

"What did you see?" Nick stroked the back of her head as he rocked her.

"I talked to Hayley."

"In your vision?"

"She's not here," Maddie said. "Her ghost isn't here."

"How do you know that?"

"She told me. She said my soul touched hers today and the only reason she came was because she was worried about me looking for her."

"It's okay," Nick said, pressing a steady stream of kisses into her hairline as he held her. "It's okay."

"She didn't die at the cabin."

"But you said ... ."

"She fell into unconsciousness there," Maddie said. "She woke up on a boat. She wasn't killed until she was on the boat. Then someone dumped her into the water."

"Did she tell you who did it?"

"It was weird. She said she was there and yet she wasn't there. She kept telling me to look at the boat."

"Tell me about the boat, my Maddie," Nick said, lulling her with small movements and soft kisses.

"It was white. It was about twenty-five feet long. It had black markings."

"Could you see a name?"

"No."

"Is there anything else?"

"No."

"Okay, Mad. I want you to let it go now."

"But ... ."

"Let it go. I'm right here. I've got you. I won't let you go. Go to sleep. I'll be right here. I'll be right here."

He quietly repeated the words over and over again until she drifted off. Then, even when he was sure sleep claimed her, he repeated them a few more times. He would always be there, and he wanted both of them – and anyone who tried to invade her dreams – to know it.

## 19. NINETEEN

"What are you doing today?" Nick asked the next morning over breakfast, pushing Maddie's still damp hair away from her face and studying her quietly. "You're pale. I need you to try and eat two lunches today. You need some fuel."

"I'm fine," Maddie said, rubbing her hand over his wrist. "You don't need to hover, and you don't need to worry all day. I promise. I'm fine."

"I need to ask about what happened last night," Nick said, serious. "How sure are you that what Hayley told you is right?"

"Very."

"Okay. I'm going to talk to John and we're going to start pulling boat registrations. I'm going to flag everything that's smaller than thirty feet. If I show you photos, do you think you can recognize the boat?"

"I have no idea," Maddie said. "Honestly ... I don't know. It was just a boat."

"It can't hurt to try," Nick said, lowering his hand and reaching for his mug of coffee. "Are you going to stay here today?"

"No."

Nick internally cringed. That was the answer he was expecting but not the one he wanted to hear. "Where are you going to go?"

"To find Michael Jarvis."

Nick stilled. "Why?"

"Hayley made me promise to deliver a message to him."

"What message?"

"I don't want to tell you," Maddie said. "I can tell just by looking at you that you're going to come up with a reason for me not to go, and I really need to go."

Nick exhaled heavily, racking his brain for a reason to talk Maddie out of her planned course of action. He couldn't come up with a single argument except his love. "Please tell me."

"They were fighting when she died," Maddie said, holding back tears. "She wanted him to know he was wrong about Trevor, but he was right about her. She wanted him to know that even though he couldn't love her like she wanted that he was the one who loved her best."

"Oh, jeez." Nick ran his hand through his hair, suddenly fighting his own tears. "You're identifying with this because it's a boy and girl being best friends, aren't you?"

"Why are you almost crying?"

"Because you are," Nick said, rubbing the heel of his hand against his cheek.

"That's not why," Maddie protested.

"Come here." Nick tugged Maddie into his arms and buried his face in her hair. "Fine. Go find Michael Jarvis. Don't go anywhere alone with him, though, and if you could find him in a public place that would be great."

"Michael isn't guilty."

"I'm sure he's not," Nick said. "I love you best, though. I need you safe."

"You do love me best."

"I always will, Maddie. I always will."

**MADDIE** kept Nick's worry – and almost tears – at the forefront of her mind as she walked down the pier. After stopping at Michael's house and being informed by his mother that he wasn't home, she'd taken a chance and headed toward the pier. Mildred said he worked at the food truck – and that was one of his favorite spots to hang out with Hayley at – so he was probably there. What better place to remember her?

"You're back."

Maddie jumped when she heard David Crowder's voice behind her. When she shifted, she couldn't keep the small smile off of her face. He was wearing the same hat, and his expression was virtually the same as it had been the other night. "I am."

"Are you looking for more witnesses?"

"I'm looking for ... a best friend."

"Isn't that who tracked you down here the other night?" David asked, lifting an eyebrow.

"He's *my* best friend," Maddie said. "I'm looking for someone else's best friend."

David pointed to the food truck behind Maddie. "He's the boy in the window," he said. "I've been watching him all day. He's in his own little world – and it's a sad world."

"He lost half of his heart."

"I think he lost more than that," David said. "Can I ask why you want to talk to him? If you think he's guilty, I can tell you that I'm pretty sure he isn't. He doesn't have it in him. You can just tell that about some people."

"I know he's not guilty," Maddie said. "I just have a message for him."

"From who?"

"The rest of his heart."

"I'm not sure what that means."

"I'm not sure you have to," Maddie said. "I'll be back in a minute."

Maddie was nervous as she approached the truck, her gaze bouncing here and there as she tried to figure out the best way to approach Michael. Up close the boy was ... despondent. His skin was sallow and his eyes were red from hours of crying. He was stoic now, but Maddie could feel his heart silently breaking from five feet away.

"Can I help you?" Michael asked, his face blank.

"I ... um ... well ... I'm here to help you."

"Help me?"

"I'm ... do you know who I am?"

"You're the psychic," Michael said. "You're Maddie Graves."

"Oh, good. You *do* know me."

"Everyone knows you," Michael said. "You're smoking hot, and when you run behind your house you wear really tiny shorts."

Maddie's face reddened. "I see."

"We all sit up on the ridge by the lake and share binoculars so we can watch you."

"I thought you were ... ."

"Gay?"

Shame flooded Maddie. "I'm sorry. That was a horrible thing to say."

"I am gay," Michael said. "My brother isn't, though, and he's a big fan of yours."

"That's possibly flattering," Maddie said. "I guess I'm going to have to start wearing longer shorts."

"Oh, don't do that," Michael said. "You'll crush the entire track team."

"I'll consider it," Maddie said. "That's not why I'm here, though."

"Are you here because you're psychic?"

Maddie tilted her head to the side, considering. "Yes." She was done feeling shame for what she was. She was bound and determined not to let it shape who she was.

Michael's face brightened. "Have you talked to Hayley?"

"In a way," Maddie said. "She's crossed over, but she wanted me to give you a message."

"What message?"

Maddie repeated Hayley's beautiful words, fighting hard to hold back tears. She didn't want to spook the boy or wound him deeper than he already was. When she was done, she couldn't help but notice that he was weeping openly – and he didn't appear to care who saw him wiping the tears away.

"She really said that?"

"She said you were the best friend she ever had."

"She's the best friend I'll ever have," Michael said. "What am I supposed to do without her?"

Maddie pursed her lips, an idea forming. "I know someone else who is hurting. He tried to protect Hayley the best way he knew how and failed. He could use a friend."

"You're talking about Trevor, aren't you?"

"He's upset, too."

"He loved her for two weeks," Michael said. "I loved her my whole life."

"There are no time limits on love," Maddie said. "You two can help each other. You can remember her together. You can love her as friends and still let her go. That's what she wants. She wants you two to be happy."

"What if I can never be happy without her?"

"Things will never be the same without her," Maddie said. "She'll always be with you, though."

"How do you know that?"

"I know a little something about having a lifelong best friend."


"THAT was a sweet thing you did for the boy."

Maddie twirled her straw in her soda and shot David a rueful smile. "How do you know what I did?"

"I was eavesdropping."

"That's illegal."

"It's not illegal," David scoffed. "It's rude, but it's not illegal."

"What did you hear?"

"I heard you admit to being psychic and then I listened as you gave that boy the one thing he desperately needed."

"Closure?"

"Forgiveness."

Maddie shifted, lifting her eyes so she could study David. "What do you mean?"

"The hardest thing in this world is being the one left behind when someone dies," David said. "What makes it worse is knowing that you said something mean to the person you love right before the unthinkable happened. You can never take that back."

"Is that what happened with your wife?"

"Yes."

"Is that why you're always out here fishing?"

"I'm out here fishing because I don't know what else to do," David said. "We planned for my retirement for thirty years. We got thirty days of it before she died. I promised to catch fish and bring them home a few times during those thirty days, but I always got distracted by the guys at the bar ... or on the golf course ... or hunting."

"Do you think you owe her fish?"

"I think I owe her ... everything," David said. "She was the love of my life, and I took it for granted."

"I'm sure she knew you were sorry," Maddie said. "Life doesn't always end with death. Sometimes there's ... more. Sometimes there's a lot more."

"I know," David said. "I'm looking forward to us sharing *more* together later. For now, though, I like to fish. It gives me a chance to think about her. She loved this lake."

"I'll bet you were a good husband."

"She was a better wife," David said. "Don't make the same mistake I did. Make sure that boy knows how much you love him every day of your life."

"I tell him every chance I get."

"Does he tell you, too?"

"Every chance he gets."

"Good," David said. "I think you two are going to have a happy life."

"I certainly hope so," Maddie said, smiling. "We started picking out paint for our bedroom last night."

"You're getting married?" David brightened. "That's a blessing."

"Not yet," Maddie said. "We've only been dating for two weeks."

"And you're already moving in together?" David was trying to refrain from frowning.

"We've loved each other as long as we've known each other," Maddie said. "We were Michael and Hayley when we were kids. We were the very best of friends."

"He's not ... you know ... is he?"

Maddie made a face. "No. That doesn't matter, though. Just because Michael is gay that doesn't mean he loved Hayley any less than she deserved."

"I didn't say it did," David said. "I just don't want anyone as pretty as you wasted on a man who can't love you with his whole heart ... and body. That would be a downright shame."

Maddie's cheeks colored. "That's ... sweet."

"I try," David said. "Why else are you down here?"

"What makes you think I'm down here for any other reason than Michael?"

"You've got a look about you," David said. "Your mind is always busy. My wife had that look. You remind me of her ... except you're tall, blonde, and about sixty pounds lighter. What else is going on?"

"Actually, I do need some more information," Maddie said. "I'm looking for a boat."

"What kind of boat?"

Maddie shrugged. "I'm not good with identifying them. I just know that the one I'm looking for is probably about twenty-five feet long. It's white and it has black markings."

David waited. When Maddie didn't continue he sent her an incredulous look. "You just described every boat on the lake."

Maddie scowled. "That's what I figured. She kept telling me to look at the boat. Look at me. Look at the boat. What do you think she meant by that?"

"Who?"

"Hayley."

"You're talking to Hayley? Isn't she dead?"

"Yes."

"She still talks to you?"

"Just the one time."

"And she told you to look at the boat?"

Maddie nodded. "Do you think that means anything?"

"It clearly means something to you," David said. He rubbed his hand across his chin thoughtfully. "You know, there is a boat out here with an odd name."

"Don't they all have odd names?"

"Most men name their boats after a woman," David said. "It could be a nice name, and it could be a nasty name. It all depends on how the big relationship in their life treated them. I once saw a boat named *True Love*."

"That's sweet."

"I also once saw a boat named *Bitter Shrew*."

Maddie snickered. "Nice. I didn't know that thing about naming your boat after a woman, though."

"It's just one of those little traditions that stuck," David said. "There is one exception on this lake. I don't know who owns it, but I do remember seeing the name and thinking only a complete and total jackass could've named it."

"What was the name?"

"*Look at Me*."

Maddie waited.

"No, that's the name of the boat," David said. "*Look at Me*."

"Oh," Maddie said, getting to her feet as realization dawned. "Oh."

"Oh," David agreed. "Do you think that's what she meant?"

"I guess we'll have to see," Maddie said, glancing around. " I need to make a call."

## 20. TWENTY

"Just so I understand what we're doing here, I want to go over it again. We're borrowing Dad's boat so we can drive around the lake because Maddie had a dream about Hayley being on a boat. That's it, right?" John asked, shoving Nick out of his spot behind the wheel. "I'm driving."

"On what planet?" Nick asked, jockeying with his older brother to regain his previous position. "You know darned well I'm a better driver than you."

"Only in your mind."

"You suck," Nick said.

"I thought you'd want a chance to snuggle with your blonde," John said, feigning innocence. "How often do you two get a chauffeured boat ride?"

Nick opened his mouth to argue and then snapped it shut. He mock saluted John and then made his way over to the seat Maddie was settled on. "I do want to snuggle with my blonde."

Maddie smiled and patted the spot next to her. "That's good. When I was having my ... dream ... last night I made a mental note to tell you that I wanted to go on a boat ride. I used to love going out on the lake with you when I was a kid. That's something we haven't done since I came back."

"Well, this doesn't count," Nick said. "When we go on a boat ride we're going to be alone, and you're going to be wearing ... far less than you are now."

"You're a smooth talker," John said, winking.

"Shut up," Nick said, making a face as he watched his brother maneuver out of the slip with precision. "You drive like a woman."

"You're prettier than a woman."

"You have hands like a woman."

"You know there's an actual woman on this boat, right?" Maddie asked. "It's kind of insulting for you two to degrade each other by using the word 'woman' as a dig."

"Oh, don't worry," Nick said, kissing Maddie's cheek. "I happen to love women."

"I've heard."

Nick grinned. "I just love one woman now."

"I'm sure that will thrill Mom," John said. "Oh, and Grandma ... and our sister ... and Aunt Tanya."

"Seriously," Nick said. "Shut up."

"I'm glad I'm an only child," Maddie said. "I've never understood why siblings always have to be fighting."

"It's because we know all the horrible buttons to push on one another," Nick said. "We can't help ourselves."

"He's right about that," John said. "For example, I know that teasing Nick about his feelings for you in high school made him cry."

"I did not cry."

"You did," John said. "You were desperate for her to love you back, and when she didn't, you curled up in your bed with a stuffed animal and cried."

"He's making that up."

Maddie was amused by their banter. "I'm not sure that works since I *did* love him back then."

"You still left him," John said.

Maddie stilled, and the look Nick shot John was murderous as he wrapped his arm around her shoulders. "Don't worry about it, Mad. Don't let him get to you."

"I'm sorry," John said, instantly contrite. "I'm guessing that's still a sore spot between the two of you. Do you want me to get you a tissue, Nick?"

"Don't bring that up again," Nick snapped, deathly serious. "We've been over it. We've talked it out. I don't want you to make her feel guilty."

"It's too late for that," Maddie said. "I feel guilty without him saying a thing."

"Thanks."

John held up his hand by way of apology. "That wasn't fair. I was trying to bug Nick. I didn't mean to hurt you, Maddie."

"I'm not sure that's true."

John glanced at her, confused. "What do you mean?"

"I think you want me out of Nick's life."

"What?" Nick was furious. "Did he say something like that to you?"

"No," John said. "I would never say something like that. I told you the other night I was jealous about what the two of you have. I would never want you to lose her, not again. I like you a lot better when you're happy rather than sad."

"Why do you think that, Mad?" Nick asked, worried

Maddie broke into a wide grin. "I don't," she said. "I just thought it might be funny if John got a taste of his own medicine."

Nick smirked, relaxing back on the seat and pulling Maddie closer to him as he shot a triumphant look in John's direction. For his part, the eldest Winters brother was incensed.

"That was a very mean thing to say, Maddie Graves," John said.

"No meaner than what you said to me."

"What I said to you was an accident."

"It was not," Maddie scoffed. "You just didn't think you'd really upset me."

"I ... how did this conversation get away from me?"

"It's because you're a moron," Nick said.

"I can't take much more of this abuse," John said.

"Do you want me to get you a tissue?" Maddie asked, her eyes sparkling.

"You're so much meaner than I remember you," John said.

"She's not mean," Nick said, kissing her cheek. "She's an angel. She's *my* angel."

"Oh, you two are just sick," John said. "Every time I turn around you're kissing each other. It's gross."

"Then don't look," Nick said. "We're never going to stop."

"I'm starting to get that," John said.

Nick pointed toward the east side of the lake. "Let's start at the hunting cabin and work our way around from there," he said. "We need a beginning point. If we're lucky, Maddie will remember something from her vision and be able to guide us where we're going."

Now it was John's turn to mock salute. "Yes, sir."

Nick rolled his eyes.

"Hold on, kids," John said, winking. "It's going to be a fast and furious ride."

"Don't hit anything," Nick said. "Dad said we had to pay for any damage we did."

"You just suck the fun out of everything," John complained. "You're a different person since you've gotten everything you've ever wanted."

"Just drive."


"OKAY," Nick said, narrowing his eyes as he studied the area surrounding the cabin. "Let's go through this. Are we sure that whoever killed Hayley approached from the lake?"

"Hayley said she would've heard a car on the dirt road in front of the cabin," Maddie said, shielding her eyes. "She said she heard so many boats on the water it never even occurred to her to worry about someone approaching from the lake."

"She told you all that and yet she couldn't tell you who killed her?" John was dubious. "I'm not sure how helpful this gift of yours is."

"I never said it was a gift."

"Oh, it's a gift," Nick said, rubbing the back of Maddie's neck. "It helped make you the best person I know, and you're a gift."

John mimed puking over the side of the boat.

"Don't make me throw you in," Nick warned.

"Let's focus," Maddie said, trying to get things back on track. "I think there's an easy answer here. It has to be her father. Have you checked to see if he has a boat?"

"I have," Nick said carefully. "There's nothing registered in his name."

"But ... ." Maddie broke off, worrying her bottom lip with her teeth. "What about her mother?"

"There's nothing listed under her name either," Nick said. "I ... ."

"You think I imagined it," Maddie said, resigned.

"No, Mad," Nick said, reaching for her. "I don't think that at all. I know you saw something important last night. I just don't think we know what it is yet."

"I think you might have imagined it," John offered. "What? Don't look at me that way, Nick. This is all new to me. I've never seen Maddie in action, and so far I'm not impressed."

Nick scowled. "I'm going to kill you."

"It's fine, Nicky," Maddie said, running her hand through her hair. "I don't blame him for not believing me."

"I think you're looking at this the wrong way, Mad," Nick said. "The fact that Hayley's parents don't have a boat could actually help us."

"How?"

Nick pursed his lips, unsure how to answer. He knew what he was about to tell her was going to throw her. "We did find someone close to Hayley who has access to a boat," Nick said.

"Who?"

"Trevor."

Maddie immediately started shaking her head. "No way. It's not him."

"I know you don't want to believe that he's capable of doing something like that," Nick said. "I think you want to believe he's innocent so you've convinced yourself that it's impossible for him to be guilty."

"I think you're talking down to me," Maddie replied, her eyes flashing. "I'm not an idiot. I don't have tunnel vision. There's no motive for Trevor. Why would he kill her?"

"Maybe she wouldn't sleep with him."

"Really? You think a teenage boy just suddenly snaps because his girlfriend won't sleep with him? He's a basketball star. If all he wanted was sex all he had to do was move on to another girl. There are plenty of girls in that school who would have slept with him."

"I understand that," Nick said, his voice calm. "Sometimes other things happen that we don't immediately understand, though."

"Whatever," Maddie said, crossing her arms over her chest. "It's not Trevor."

"Okay," Nick said, holding his hands up. "Maybe someone with a boat saw Hayley outside of the cabin one day. Maybe whoever went after her has nothing to do with the situation that got her into this mess in the first place."

"Speaking of that mess, why haven't you questioned her father about beating her yet?"

"I wanted more information first," Nick said, fighting hard to tamp down his anger. Maddie was starting to get belligerent, and the last thing he wanted was a full-blown fight. "Once we haul him in and tell him what we know he's liable to lawyer up. We don't want to tip him off until we have more information."

Maddie's eyes glittered with tears, this time out of frustration instead of sadness. "I'm sorry. You're right."

Nick grabbed her and pulled her to him, resting his face against the side of her head. "I don't know what to do here, Mad. I know what you saw ... but the evidence seems to be pointing away from the parents."

"But what about ... *Look at Me*."

Nick focused on Maddie, his eyes plaintive. When she didn't expand he tilted his head to the side. "I'm looking at you."

"Ugh, David was right about that being a stupid name for a boat,"

Maddie said. "I don't want you to look at me. There's a boat out here named *Look at Me*."

"Okay," Nick said. "I don't know why that's important."

"Hayley kept telling me to look at the boat," Maddie said. "She kept repeating it over and over again."

Nick rubbed the heel of his hand against his forehead and exhaled heavily. "We can run the name of the boat." He exchanged a quick look with John before moving to the bag on the other side of the deck. He pulled out his laptop and booted it up, engaging the mobile hub on his cell phone and logging into the registration database. "Just hold on a second. It might take a little longer to do the search out here because my signal isn't very strong."

Maddie paced to the far side of the boat, her gaze trained on the placid water. John took the opportunity to move to Nick's side. "She's really serious about this."

"Why do you think I'm running the boat?"

"I think you don't want to fight with her," John said.

"I don't. I ... ." The computer dinged as the search results returned. "Here it is."

"Who does it belong to?" John asked. "It has to be a narcissist."

"Does Marla have a boat?" Maddie asked, bitter.

"The boat doesn't belong to Marla," Nick said, his shoulders stiffening.

"Who does it belong to?"

"Shelly Watkins."

"Who is that?" John asked.

"She's Jessica Watkins' mother."

John waited.

"Jessica Watkins married Andrew Walker. They're the proud – and grieving – parents of Hayley Walker."

John sucked in a breath. "Bingo. Maddie was right."

"She always is," Nick said, raising his eyes to Maddie's. He expected to see anger there, maybe even some triumph. She'd earned it. Instead, he saw relief. That's when he realized what was really bothering her. She'd been wondering if the vision was nothing more than a bad dream, too. "You were right, love."

"Now can we go talk to Hayley's father?"

"You bet your cute little butt we can. Come sit down next to me. I want to snuggle with you again while John taxies us back to the dock."

Once Maddie was settled next to him, Nick kissed her lightly. "You can tell me that you told me so."

"I don't care about that," Maddie said. "You believe in me. That's all I care about."

"I could never believe in anyone but you, Maddie. Never. I'm still sorry."

"You can make it up to me with a massage later," Maddie said.

"As long as you don't make me choose paint again I'll rub you for the rest of my life."

"You two are filthy," John said.

"Drive!"

## 21. TWENTY-ONE

"Okay, here's the deal, Mad," Nick said, raising his hand to knock on the front of the Walkers' door. "You need to be quiet. If they ask who you are just say you're a consultant. You can't ask any questions. Do you understand?"

"What if I think you're asking the wrong questions?"

"I ... you can't," Nick said. "We need to do this by the book. You being here might make the parents jumpy. You have a certain reputation in this town."

"And that was before you started fornicating with my brother like a horny little bunny," John said.

Maddie narrowed her eyes and glared and John. "I'm going to be the one who beats you up when we're done here."

"You're cute," John said. "While I might find it hot to have you ... smack me around a little ... I'm not sure my brother would like that."

Nick rolled his eyes, nonplussed. "You remember she's an athlete, right? She's stronger than she looks, and she'll fight dirty if she needs to."

"Are you losing a lot of pillow fights to her?"

"Those aren't losses," Nick said. "They're ... draws."

John grinned. "Sick, sick, sick."

"Whatever," Nick said. "Just ... I need you to promise me you're not going to ask any questions."

"Okay," Maddie said, nodding. "Can I touch things?"

"You can touch me," John offered.

"I will hold you down while she beats you," Nick said.

"I mean ... can I touch things in the house?" Maddie asked, ignoring John's attempt at humor. "I might get a flash of something."

"Are you going to stop breathing on me?"

"No."

"Then you can touch things as long as they're not looking," Nick said. "In fact ... I'm going to try and isolate them in the kitchen. See if you can find Hayley's room. Touch away. Just don't let anyone catch you doing it."

"That's not going to be admissible in court," John said.

"We're not looking for testimony in court," Nick said. "I just want Maddie to get some insight into the right questions to ask if she can. If you get something, come down and stand in the doorway. Cough. I'll come to you."

"I know. You'll drop everything and come running."

Nick smiled. "Always." He kissed her lightly.

"I'm seriously going to puke," John said.

"Everyone put their poker faces on," Nick said. "Here we go."


"**THANK YOU** for seeing us," Nick said, forcing his face to remain even as he sat in one of the kitchen chairs and watched Jessica and Andrew Walker.

"Do you have information on Hayley's death?" Andrew asked, sipping from a beer. Since it was barely three, Nick wanted to call the man on his drinking, but he didn't think it was his place. They still weren't sure he was guilty, and people grieve in different ways.

"Some things have come to light," Nick said, choosing his words carefully. "First off, we know where Hayley was staying for the past two weeks."

"Where?" Jessica asked, immediately shifting her wary eyes toward her husband. She was scared of him. That much was obvious.

"Were you aware she was dating Trevor Gardner?"

"The basketball player?" Andrew asked.

"Yes."

"I didn't think she'd be pretty enough to snag a sports stud, but good for her," Andrew said.

Nick narrowed his eyes. "They dated a few weeks, and then Hayley approached Trevor with a problem she was having."

"Which was?"

"She said you were beating her," John said, his voice flat.

Andrew slammed his hands down on the table angrily, causing his wife to flinch and cover her face. "That is a lie!"

"Mr. Walker, you need to calm down," Nick said. "Trevor saw numerous bruises on Hayley's arms and ribcage. She told him you gave her those bruises."

"Well, they weren't from me," Andrew said. "I was a good father."

"Clearly," John said. "I think a good father always lets his daughter run away for two weeks and doesn't lift a finger to find her."

"You have no idea what you're talking about," Andrew said. "If you're here to accuse me of doing something to her ... you can just get out of my house right now."

"That's certainly your prerogative," Nick said, calm. "If that's what you want, then we'll be taking you into custody and finishing our questioning at the police station. Is that what you want?"

"You don't have any evidence against me," Andrew scoffed. "You can't arrest me."

"I think you'd be surprised by the evidence we've uncovered," Nick said, choosing his words carefully.

"Are you saying I'm a suspect?"

"I'm saying we need some information from you and you're going to give it to us."

Andrew made a face and crossed his arms over his chest. "What do you want to know?"

"How many times did you beat Hayley?"

"I never laid a hand on that girl," Andrew charged. "Ask my wife. She'll tell you."

"Is that true, Mrs. Walker?"

Jessica stared down at her hands, her face unreadable. "My husband is a good man."

"Even a good man can lose his temper," John said. "Have you ever seen your husband lose his temper?"

"Of course not." She was clearly lying ... and terrified.

"Is that all?" Andrew asked.

"No," Nick said. "I need to know when you last borrowed Mrs. Watkins' boat."

Andrew seemed surprised by the question, and Jessica's only response was to clasp her hands together tightly on top of the table. "I haven't been out on that boat in at least five years. I'm not much of a boater."

"I see," Nick said. "What would you say if I told you that someone saw your mother-in-law's boat outside of the Gardner cabin the day Hayley was killed?"

"I would say I don't know how that matters," Andrew said. "Is that where Hayley was staying?"

"You're saying you didn't know where she was staying?" John pressed.

"I'm saying I had no idea where she was staying," Andrew shot back. "I thought she was at a girlfriend's house ... or with that freak Jarvis kid she insisted on being friends with. I didn't even know she was dating the Gardner boy."

"I find that hard to believe," Nick said.

"I find it hard to believe you're a police officer," Andrew said.

"Here's what's going to happen," Nick said, gritting his teeth to keep from lashing out. "We're going to confiscate Mrs. Watkins' boat and have a tech team go over every inch of it. We've already gathered evidence from the cabin, where there were obvious signs of a struggle. Between you beating Hayley, and the other evidence, things aren't looking good for you."

"I did not beat my daughter!" Andrew hit the table with such force his wife practically ducked underneath it to protect herself. Nick's heart went out to her. She'd lost her daughter, and now her husband was coming unhinged.

"Mrs. Walker, I think it might be a good idea if you found another place to stay for a few days," Nick said. "Your husband seems to be having trouble ... controlling his emotions."

"She's not going anywhere," Andrew seethed. "Don't you even think about breaking up my family."

"I think you've done that yourself, sir."

"Really? How come you're not taking me into custody then?"

"We're still collecting evidence," Nick replied. Movement in the doorway caught his attention, and when he shifted his eyes to Maddie she imperceptibly shook her head. She hadn't found anything. That was disheartening. "When we complete our investigation, you'll be the first to know."

Nick turned back to Jessica. "Are you sure you don't want us to give you a ride somewhere?"

"I belong with my husband," Jessica said, her voice weak. "He's a good man."

That was a mantra Andrew had apparently drilled into his wife's head. Nick pushed himself up from the table. "We'll be in touch."

"I'm getting a lawyer," Andrew said.

"I think that's probably a good idea."


"THAT could have gone better," John said when the three of them were back outside and standing by Nick's Explorer.

"It could've gone worse, too," Nick said.

"I'm not sure how."

"They didn't give you anything?" Maddie asked.

"We got a couple of impressive table beatdowns from the husband," John said. "The wife sat there shaking like a leaf. He's obviously beating her, too."

"Did he admit to beating Hayley?"

"He's a good man," John and Nick said in unison.

"I ... ."

"It's something his wife kept saying," Nick said. "She kept repeating it every time we asked her a question."

"I don't think it's safe for her to stay in this house," Maddie said.

"I don't think it is either," Nick said. "We can't make her leave, though. She says she wants to stay."

"Can't you arrest him?"

"Not without more evidence, Mad," Nick said. "We have to take this one step at a time."

"What's the next step?"

"We're impounding the boat," Nick said, glancing at John. "You should probably get on that right now."

John nodded. "Leave it to me. We'll have it in two hours. They won't have time to get rid of any evidence."

"I'm sure they've already hosed it down."

"We might get lucky." John pulled his cell phone out of his pocket and started walking toward the end of the driveway. "Give me five minutes."

Nick nodded. Once his brother was gone he fixed his eyes on Maddie. "You didn't get anything?"

"There's nothing there," Maddie said. "I found a bedroom that clearly belonged to Hayley, but it was ... empty."

"What do you mean?"

"There was a bed and a desk ... and a few stuffed animals ... but everything else was gone. I touched what was there, but nothing seemed to feel like it belonged to Hayley. It felt more like a spare room than anything else."

"Do you think they already cleaned the room out?"

"I think that room was never really a home to Hayley," Maddie said. "I think Hayley had a worse childhood than we thought. I think ... she was never loved by that man."

Nick ran his tongue over his teeth, fighting the urge to hold Maddie while Andrew might be watching from inside of the house. "I don't know what else to do for Jessica Walker right now. I don't like leaving her here. I've got a bad feeling about it. There's just nothing I can do."

Maddie rubbed the tender spot between her eyebrows. "I might be able to do something."

"What?"

"I know someone who can watch Mrs. Walker without anyone noticing," Maddie said.

"If you suggest Maude we're breaking up."

Maddie made a face.

"I'm lying," Nick said, forcing a tight smile onto his face. "I'd never break up with you. We still can't use Maude, and if you even suggest volunteering to do it yourself I'm tying you to the bed until this case is over with."

"Nice," Maddie said, annoyed.

"I'll bring you food and water and do a striptease for you every night."

"I wasn't talking about Granny, and I wasn't talking about me," Maddie said.

"Who were you talking about?"

"Mom."

Nick stilled. He'd never even considered that. "Can you do that? Can you ask your mother to watch over the living? I thought she couldn't control when she popped up."

"She's getting stronger," Maddie said. "I'm not guaranteeing she can do it, and she doesn't always come when I call, but I can ask her. I do think she's our best option. If something bad happens, she will be able to warn us. When I tell her what's going on she's going to want to help."

"Okay," Nick said. "Let's try it."

His enthusiasm surprised Maddie. "Really?"

"We have nothing to lose here, Mad," Nick said. "I have faith in you. You haven't led me astray once. You've been right at every turn."

"What happens if I'm wrong?"

"Then we're not out anything," Nick said. "We don't have to tell anyone what you're doing – especially my brother – and we'll just keep it between the two of us for right now."

"I don't blame you for being embarrassed."

"I'm not embarrassed," Nick said. "It's just not something I want you opening yourself up to. Not right now."

"Are you sure?"

"I'm sure I love you more than anything in this world," Nick said. "I'm also sure we'll feel better about your mom watching over Jessica while we try to gather evidence. This is clearly our best option."

"I really do love you," Maddie said, beaming. "I would love to be able to hug you right now."

Nick smirked, reaching for her without giving it another thought.

"What if Andrew Walker is watching?" Maddie asked, squirming.

"I don't care," Nick said. "If he wants to tell someone that I was hugging the most beautiful woman in the world in his driveway I think that's something I can live with."

"Okay, you officially are a smooth talker," Maddie said, giving up the fight and resting her head against his chest.

"I have my moments," Nick agreed.

At the end of the driveway, John disconnected his phone and turned back to Maddie and Nick, his thumb in the air to signify "mission accomplished." When he saw the couple cuddled together his face twisted. "Seriously? Sick!"

## 22. TWENTY-TWO

"Did you get it?"

Nick hopped out of his Explorer and started moving toward John. After separating at the police station, Nick dropping his brother off so he could collect his vehicle, Nick took Maddie home so she could talk to Olivia and then headed straight for the marina. He wanted to be there when the tech team searched the boat.

"I got it," John said, lifting the folded search warrant. "We're good to go."

"Was it hard?"

"Not really," John said. "Judge Mitchell is keen for this case to be solved. No one likes it when a teenager is murdered, especially in a community this small. Where is Maddie?"

"I took her home," Nick said, being careful not to tip his hand. While John had been gracious and kind (for the most part) where Maddie's abilities were concerned, there was no way Nick was owning up to letting Maddie ask a ghost to help them solve a crime. He wasn't keen on opening himself up to ridicule, but he was adamant he would never allow Maddie to undergo one second of it if he could help it. This was a case of him being able to control the situation. "She wanted to check on Maude."

"Are you serious? I thought for sure she'd be all over this."

"Once we get the boat into the garage to search it I told her I would call her so she could come down," Nick said.

"Are you going to let her touch it?"

"I'm going to see how many people are around first," Nick said, keeping his eyes on the tech team as they gathered their supplies out of a state issued van.

"You're handling this really well," John said. "I'm not sure how I would take something like that. I mean ... didn't you ever doubt she could do what she said she could do?"

"Not really," Nick said. "She hasn't been wrong and ... well ... something happened one of the first nights right after she came back."

John waited.

"We were at the festival downtown," Nick said. "Maddie and I weren't really in a good place. I'd seen her exactly twice and it was ... rough."

"Because you knew you were still in love with her and you didn't want to be?" John asked.

"Yes," Nick said. "I honestly knew the second I saw her. I just couldn't ... process it. Anyway, I was at the concert in town square ... and Cassidy was there and I was trying really hard not to talk to her because I'd already ... ."

"Tossed her away like yesterday's newspaper?"

"Mentally? Yes. I know that's horrible to say, but I was distancing myself from her before Maddie came back," Nick said. "I was hoping she would break up with me. Once I saw Maddie, though, it really was over. I was really horrible to Cassidy."

"You can't go back in time and fix it," John said. "You and Maddie are happy. Heck, you and Maddie are so happy it literally makes me want to puke."

"Literally?"

"Yes."

Nick rolled his eyes. "Anyway, I happened to see Maddie up at one of the food trucks with Christy and she suddenly just ... bent over. I thought she was getting sick."

"Tell me the truth, did you run to her?"

"Yes," Nick said, guileless. "Her face was all red, and she was sweating and shaking. I was scared for her. Then she started walking. I kept telling her to sit down, but she refused. She was really focused. She took me five blocks away from the festival, turning around twice because she decided we were going the wrong way. All the while she was physically ill."

"Don't keep me in suspense, man."

"She led me to a missing child," Nick said. "The kid was huddled behind a car and crying. She was lost. She wasn't in any immediate danger, but she was really upset."

"Is that when you knew?"

"That's when things started ... slipping into place," Nick replied. "I started thinking about all the time we spent together as kids and ... I just ... you look at things differently when you're an adult."

"Do you feel stupid for not realizing it?"

"I feel stupid for not realizing she was going through some major stuff," Nick said. "I was too self-absorbed."

"I don't think that was the problem," John said. "You were always very aware of what Maddie was thinking and feeling. I thought it was weird when we were younger. You doted on her even then, though."

"I didn't dote on her," Nick protested.

"Yes, you did," John said. "Mom and Olivia used to talk about it when you two weren't around. They thought it was adorable. They were both planning a big wedding in their heads."

"And then things fell apart," Nick mused.

"Then things took a turn," John said. "You guys came full circle and worked everything out, though. Given how great things are now, would you change anything?"

"No," Nick said. "She's my ... Maddie."

John rolled his eyes. "Sick."

"Come on," Nick said. "No offense to you, and it has been nice to see more of you over the past few days, but the sooner we get this case finished the sooner I can take Maddie for a picnic, and a boat ride, and a moonlight swim, and ... ."

"Seriously, man, you're not animals," John said, chuckling.

"It's not about *that*," Nick said, making a face. "It's about ... spending time with her."

"It's a little about that," John said. "Admit it."

"No."

"Admit it or I'll wrestle you down in front of the tech team and give you a wedgie until you do admit it."

Nick scowled. "Don't ruin my happiness."

"I don't want to ruin your happiness," John said. "I just like to mess with you. You make it so easy."

"Whatever," Nick said, stalking away from his Explorer. "Let's go search a boat."

One of the tech team members stepped into Nick's path and held up a hand. "We have a problem."

"What's wrong?" Nick asked, instantly alert.

"The boat you asked us to search, the ... *Look At Me* ... who names their boat that, by the way?"

"What about it?" Nick asked.

"It's gone."

"What?"

"It's gone," the tech said. "According to the dockhand someone drove it out of here not more than fifteen minutes ago. He didn't see who it was, though. He just heard the engine and saw the boat leaving."

"Sonovabitch," Nick swore. "Andrew Walker beat us here. We should have thought about that."

"Calm down," John said. "It's a small lake, not a big ocean. There are only so many places he can go. We'll find him. First we need to organize a search. Come on."

"HI," Maddie said, greeting David Crowder with a wide smile as she handed him a Tupperware container full of chocolate chip cookies.

David took the cookies with a curious expression. "What's this for?"

"You helped me," Maddie said. "I wanted to do something nice for you."

"You baked me cookies?"

"My grandmother baked the cookies," Maddie said. "I just stole them."

"Maude is your grandmother, isn't she?"

"You know Granny?"

"I know she doesn't like that you call her that."

Maddie grinned. "She's told me. She does make outstanding cookies."

"Not that I'm complaining, but can I ask why you decided to reward me with cookies?" David asked.

"I just thought you looked like you might like some cookies."

"My wife used to make me fresh cookies all the time," David said, his face thoughtful. "I haven't had a chance to eat any since ... well ... it's been a long time."

Maddie didn't know how she knew that, but she knew it. After searching the house for Olivia – and coming up empty – she'd decided to cross another task off her list, and that task happened to involve David. "I guess they came at a good time then."

"I think you might have come around at a good time," David said. "Tell me about the boat. Did you find it? Does it have something to do with Hayley's death?"

"We did find it," Maddie said. "Nick and his brother are down at the marina serving a search warrant and taking it into custody right now." Maddie pointed about a half mile down the beach, and even though it was a decent ways away the swirling police lights were bright as they bounced across the choppy water.

"Who does it belong to?"

"Hayley Walker's grandmother."

David frowned. "Her grandmother killed her?"

"No," Maddie said. "We're not a hundred-percent-sure who killed her, but odds are it was her father. He was ... mistreating her."

David scowled. "Really? Her own father?"

"He's got issues," Maddie said. "Nick thinks he's mistreating his wife, too."

"That's a shame," David said. "I had no idea that girl was going through so much. I can't help but think ... ."

"If you'd known you would have tried to help her," Maddie finished for him. "I know. Do you have children?"

"We were never blessed that way," David said. "Sometimes I wish we would have adopted ... maybe taken in a kid who needed help."

Maddie glanced over her shoulder, her gaze landing on Michael as he worked behind the counter of the food truck. He was the real reason she was here. "It's probably too late to adopt now," she said. "It's not too late to help a child in pain, though."

David shifted his attention to Michael. "He seems to be doing okay."

"He's struggling," Maddie said. "Something tells me you already know that. That's why you're fishing here."

"The fishing happens to be really good here," David said, shifting from one foot to the other.

"Really?" Maddie gestured toward David's empty bucket. "You forget, I know about fishing. I haven't done it in a little while, but I know about it. It's too shallow and choppy right here. You're not catching anything. You're hanging out here to keep an eye on Michael. Don't bother denying it."

"He's a good kid," David said. "I just ... sense I'm needed here for some reason."

Maddie knew a little about sensing things. "You're a very good man."

"Oh, good grief, don't get all mushy," David said. "I'm not doing anything any other decent person wouldn't do."

"I don't believe that," Maddie said. "If you want to keep this ... curmudgeonly ... exterior up, though, go for it. Just keep in mind, someone like you might have a lot to offer a kid who has lost the most important person in his life."

David's face softened. "I ... ."

"You don't have to say anything," Maddie said, tentatively touching his arm. "Just think about it."

"People don't tell you no very often, do they?"

"I think it depends on the person."

"That boyfriend of yours never tells you no. I can tell that."

"He tells me no," Maddie said.

"When?"

"I ... ."

"That's what I thought," David said, grinning. "He's so in love with you he would rob a bank to make you happy."

"He's a police officer. He would never rob a bank. He has very specific ideas about what is right and what is wrong."

"You two seem like you're a good fit."

"We do our best," Maddie said, lifting her head as the breeze started to pick up. "It's getting cold."

"A storm is coming," David said. "I saw the weather report earlier. It's going to be a big one. I thought it would hold off for another couple hours, but that doesn't seem to be the case."

"I guess I should get moving and go down to the marina," Maddie said. "I promised Nick I would meet him for dinner and then he's going to take me to some garage where they're going to search the boat."

"Be careful," David cautioned. "I think this storm is going to be a dilly."

"Then I should definitely get going," Maddie said. "I promise to stop back as soon as I have time. I'm going to want to give Michael an update ... and maybe even see if you've managed to catch some fish."

"I'll have you know I'm an excellent fisherman."

"You're a good man. That's all that matters."

Maddie left David to his empty bucket and big heart and started moving down the pier. When she got close to the parking lot, a flash of something white caught her attention out of the corner of her eye. She slowed her pace and peered into a thick grove of trees down the beach. There was something there, she realized. Her inner senses started prickling – and that always meant something was up. Without thinking what she was doing Maddie swerved away from the parking lot and headed toward the trees.

It couldn't hurt to look. She had time. The storm was still a little ways away. It wouldn't take more than a few minutes. She would just look and then hurry to Nick. It would bother her if she didn't at least take a look. It was probably nothing.

She had no idea just how wrong she was about to be.

## 23. TWENTY-THREE

Nick pounded on the front door of the Walker home. This was his third round. He was worried Jessica Walker was either hurt or ... something worse. He was going to give it one more round before kicking the door in.

Just as he raised his hand one more time the door flew open. Instead of a cowering – or bleeding – Jessica, though, Nick found a fuming Andrew Walker staring at him from the other side of the threshold.

"What the ... ?" Andrew's face contorted. "Is there a reason you're beating on my door? Do you need attention? I told you two hours ago that I was getting a lawyer. If you want to talk to me again then you go through him."

Nick faltered. "I ... have you been here all afternoon?"

"Yes."

"Alone?"

Andrew lifted his half-empty bottle of Jack Daniels. "Just me and my bud here."

Nick and John exchanged a look. "Mr. Andrews, can anyone confirm your whereabouts this afternoon?"

"Just Jack," Andrew said, slurring slightly as he turned and shuffled back into his house.

Even though they hadn't been invited Nick and John followed. They were both worried about Jessica Walker's current status, and this was the best way they could think of to find out if she was okay.

Andrew didn't stop until he reached the kitchen, which looked the same as the last time they'd been in the room. Thankfully, there were no signs of a struggle. "Can I get you two a drink?"

"We're on duty," John said.

"So?"

"We can't drink on duty."

"Your loss." Andrew unscrewed the cap on the bottle and drank directly from it. "Good stuff."

"Mr. Walker, where is your wife?" Nick asked pointedly.

"She went out," Andrew said. "She had to make arrangements for Hayley's funeral. She's making a big deal out of it. I told her it was a waste of time. She's dead. She doesn't care."

John scowled. "I'm sure *you* would see it that way."

"What other way is there to see it?" Andrew asked. "She ran away from home and got herself killed. I don't see why we should reward bad behavior. I'm not wasting money on a funeral when we don't have it to spend."

Nick was overwhelmed with the sudden urge to hit the man. If he'd been alone, he wasn't sure if he would have been able to stop himself. "Can we search your home to make sure that your wife is really ... out?"

Andrew made a face. "Why would you want to search my house?"

"We're worried about your wife," Nick said. "You were ... aggressive ... when we left."

"And you think I hurt my wife? Of course, you do. You think I beat my daughter. Why wouldn't you think I beat my wife, too."

"I'm going to look around the house," John said. "You're going to ... stay right here with my brother while I look. Do you understand?"

"I'm not stupid," Andrew said.

Nick wasn't so sure. "Go," he said. "Mr. Walker and I are going to have a little talk here."

"I'm sure that's going to be illuminating."

. . .

**MADDIE** tried to tuck her hair behind her ears as the wind swirled around her. The storm was coming ... and it was coming fast. She didn't have a lot of time, and yet something inside was telling her that she had to find what was hidden behind the trees.

After picking her way through the dense underbrush, Maddie found herself standing in front of a small boat. The front end of the craft was tied off to one of the trees, and it was starting to buck up and down as the wind whipped the water into a frenzy.

Maddie circled the boat until she got to the far side, and her eyebrows flew up when she read the name of the boat: *Look At Me.*

Holy crap.

Maddie dug into her pocket to find her phone, pulling it out of her pocket and focusing on the screen. Instead of making a call, which would call attention to her presence if someone was under the deck, she decided to send a text. After typing out a few cursory words – including her location – Maddie pressed "send" and pocketed the phone. Nick was close. He would be here soon. That meant she had time to get a better look at the boat before the storm hit. She wouldn't be out here alone for long.

After studying the boat for a few minutes, taking the time to move from one side to the other and then back again, Maddie made a decision: She had to see what – if anything – was on board. She had to know if it was the same boat she'd dreamed about. She had to know if this was where Hayley died.

Maddie waded into the water, internally thankful she was wearing her J-41 shoes so it didn't matter if they got wet, and quietly moved toward the boat. Since the wind was busy the water was already lapping at the shore and making a decent amount of noise. If someone was on the boat they wouldn't hear her approach.

Maddie's hand was already on the ladder when an inner voice urged her to turn around. The voice belonged to Nick, and he was begging her to think. She yanked her hand back, worrying her bottom lip with her teeth as she considered what to do. Climbing onto this boat – a boat she was pretty sure had been used to dump a teenage girl's dead body into the lake – was a bad idea. If she could be assured the boat was empty, that would change things.

"Hello?"

No one answered.

Maddie cleared her throat and tried again, a little louder this time. "Hello?"

When no one answered again Maddie beat her hands on the side of the boat for good measure. "Hello!"

The boat was empty. Maddie was sure of it. She made up her mind quickly. She raised her hand to the ladder and swung herself up. She had to look around before the storm washed all potential evidence from the vessel. She just had to see. She was convinced Andrew Walker had abandoned it here – knowing full well the storm was rolling in and would wash all trace evidence away – and that meant she had to look around before it was too late.

What was the harm? Nick was on his way, after all.

"MR. WALKER, were you aware that your mother-in-law's boat was removed from the marina about an hour ago?"

Andrew raised his eyebrows. "No. Why should I know that? It's not my boat."

"I just find it suspicious that right after we told you we were impounding the boat it went missing."

"I obviously didn't take it," Andrew said. "I don't even know how to drive a boat. Jessica tried to teach me, but she doesn't have a lot of patience. It's harder than it looks."

Nick wrinkled his nose. "Jessica doesn't have a lot of patience?"

"She always said she wanted to be a teacher, but she would've killed all of her students on the first day," Andrew said. "She doesn't like it when people talk back to her."

"I guess that's a family trait," Nick said.

"What are you getting at?"

"Mr. Walker, I don't know who you're trying to fool, but I saw your temper on display this afternoon," Nick said. "Do you think I'm stupid enough to believe you keep your hands to yourself? People saw the bruises on Hayley. Just ... stop."

Instead of reacting in anger, like Nick was expecting, Andrew's eyes filled with tears. "If you think I don't know what I did to Hayley was wrong ... then you *are* the stupid one," he said. "I ... I know what I did. I'm not proud of it."

Nick faltered. "What did you do?"

"I hit her," Andrew admitted. "I hit her more than once. I hit her hard. She was always talking back. She was always ... obnoxious. I hit her. I admit it. I hit her and ... I ... hurt her."

"How did you hurt her?"

"I didn't mean to do it," Andrew said. "Something's broken inside of me. I'm a horrible man. I'm a deviant. I'm sick. I blame it on the liquor. It turned me into a ... demon."

Nick's heart rolled painfully. It was time to ask the one question everyone had been skirting around for days. "Did you rape your daughter?"

"It only happened once," Andrew said. "I ... I was drunk. I was confused. I didn't mean for it to happen. I just couldn't stop myself."

Bile climbed up Nick's throat. "She was your daughter."

"I just got confused," Andrew said. "I apologized for what I did. I was going to get ... help. I was going to go into rehab. I knew that what I was doing was wrong. I just ... she shouldn't have enticed me that way. She was asking for it."

Revulsion washed over Nick, followed quickly by rage. "Mr. Walker, please step away from the counter."

"What? Why?"

"You're under arrest," Nick said.

"You should just let me kill myself," Andrew said, his face serious. "I have nothing left to live for anyway."

"I don't think your future is going to be that easy," Nick said, reaching for the cuffs on his belt. "Put your hands out in front of you and step away from the counter. You're under arrest."

. . .

**MADDIE** searched the deck of the boat before poking her head into the cabin beneath. It was a small room, and thankfully it was empty. She'd been right. Someone abandoned the boat here hoping to take advantage of the storm.

A far off rumble of thunder told Maddie the tempest was getting closer, which meant she was running out of time. She turned her attention back to the deck, screwing her eyes shut and trying to step back into the vision. After a few moments, Maddie moved to the side of the boat where she believed Hayley had been resting in the vision and knelt down, pressing her fingertips to the fiberglass floor and hoping for a flash.

Nothing.

Frustration bubbled up, and Maddie fought to tamp it down as she busily slowed her eyes so she could scan each small portion of the deck in a methodical way. Her gaze landed on something underneath the bench on the aft side, and she crawled toward, something calling to her.

She couldn't reach it until she flattened her body on the deck and extended her arm – and then the second her fingertips made contact with the item, which she realized now was a nylon rope, darkness overtook her and she slipped into someone else's nightmare.

*Hayley.*


"WHAT'S going on?" John asked, walking back into the kitchen and fixing Nick and Andrew with a surprised look. "Are we taking him into custody? I thought ... ."

"I just read him his rights," Nick said. "He admitted beating ... and raping ... Hayley."

John's face drained of color. "What?"

"It was an accident," Andrew spat. "I didn't mean to do it."

"Yeah, you accidentally climbed into your daughter's bed and raped her while she was kicking and screaming," Nick said, disgustedly yanking the cuffs tighter. "Shut up."

"They're too tight," Andrew whined.

"Shut up," John said.

"Did you find his wife?" Nick asked, inclining his head toward the hallway John had just emerged from.

"She's not here," John said. "I can't find her purse, and there's only one vehicle in the garage. I think she might actually be out."

Nick stilled. "Really? I thought for sure … ."

"You're not the only one," John said. "I had a thought about that, though. What if Andrew forced her to move the boat? If he wasn't seen on it, that would give him an alibi for Hayley's death. He could claim someone else stole the boat and have plausible deniability."

That was an interesting idea. Nick turned back to Andrew. "Is that what happened? Did you make your wife steal the boat?"

"No one makes my wife do anything," Andrew said, bitter. "Why do you think I had to look elsewhere for some love?"

"I'm going to hit you," Nick hissed. "I … you make me sick."

"Let's take him down to the station," John said. "We need to get him processed, and we need him to give us the details on how he killed Hayley and why he dumped her in the lake. It's going to be a long night."

"I didn't kill Hayley," Andrew said, incensed. "I already told you that."

"You also told me you didn't beat her," Nick replied, nonplussed. "Forgive me if I don't take you at your word."

"Fine. I lied about that," Andrew said, frustrated. "I'm not lying about this, though. Why would I kill Hayley? She was all I had."

"What about your wife?"

"My wife is a cold and bitter woman," Andrew said.

"Is that why you beat her?"

"I don't beat her," Andrew said. "I'd never lay a hand on her. I'm too scared. She's one of those women who will cut your junk off when you're sleeping. We don't even share the same bedroom."

Something about Andrew's admission niggled at the back of Nick's mind. "What? Do you sleep on the couch?"

"No. I sleep in the master bedroom and she sleeps in the other bedroom. It down the hall from mine."

"But ... I ... this is only a two-bedroom house," Nick said, confused. "If your wife slept in the second bedroom, where did Hayley sleep?"

"There's another bedroom in the basement," Andrew said. "That's where Hayley stayed. It's a small bedroom ... and it's isolated. It made things easier."

"You're one sick bastard," John said. "That's it. I've had enough of you. I have a feeling you're going to be very popular in prison when word gets out about what you've done."

Andrew's face blanched. "That's so unfair!"

"That's what happens when you rape and kill your daughter," John spat.

"I did not kill Hayley! How many times do I have to tell you that?"

"Then who did?"

## 24. TWENTY-FOUR

Maddie rested her head against her knees as she leaned her back on the bench, horror washing over her. Hayley's death had been worse than she thought ... so much worse. She was having trouble absorbing the horror of the teen's last moments.

Maddie was so caught up in her thoughts – and Hayley's final memories – that she didn't recognize the unmistakable sounds of someone climbing the boat ladder and landing on the deck.

"Why am I not surprised?"

Maddie jerked her head up, the color draining from her face as she met Jessica Walker's terrible green eyes. "You killed your daughter."

Jessica didn't seem surprised by the statement, haphazardly dropping a bag of food on the deck as she regarded Maddie with blasé indifference. "Someone had to do it."

"But ... why?"

"She was going to go to the police," Jessica said. "Do you have any idea what that would have done to my family? Do you have any idea how embarrassing that would have been?"

"You let your husband beat her," Maddie said hollowly. "You knew he was beating her. You didn't stop him."

"There was only so much I could do," Jessica said. "I didn't want him to start in on me. That's why I moved to the second bedroom. The man has issues. What can I say?"

"That's not even the worst thing you did," Maddie said, her stomach roiling. "You knew he raped her and you not only didn't say anything, but you were purposely complicit in wanting her to keep quiet about it."

"How can you possibly know that?" Jessica asked, narrowing her eyes. "No one knows that. There's no way Andrew would've told you. He climbed into a bottle weeks ago, and now he's making noises about killing himself. Personally, I hope he does it. That's going to make things a lot easier on me."

Maddie knew she was in a sticky situation, but since she was in such a vulnerable position on the ground – and Jessica was in a superior position while standing – she decided to take things slowly. Nick was on his way. She just had to keep Jessica talking. She had to distract her.

"When did you find out that your husband raped your daughter?"

Jessica didn't appear bothered by the question. "I heard him while he was doing it. The screaming was … ridiculous."

"And you didn't stop him? Why didn't you save her?"

"Hey, as long as he wasn't trying to touch me … ." Jessica made a disgusted face. "Do you have any idea how gross he looks without a shirt on? It's really too bad. He was handsome when I married him. That's why I agreed to go out with him in the first place.

"My mother told me he was beneath me when I first brought him home," she continued. "I didn't want to believe her. He was so handsome, and he had big dreams. Here's a tip: Big dreams don't equate to big outcomes. I should have realized he wasn't smart enough to make those dreams come true."

"Why didn't you just divorce him?"

"I'm a Watkins," Jessica said, straightening her shoulders. "We don't get divorced. No one in my family has ever gotten divorced."

"So, instead of putting up with the stigma of being divorced you decided to let your husband brutalize your daughter and keep quiet about it," Maddie supplied. "You should be named Mother of the Year."

"Oh, get over yourself," Jessica said. "My daughter was never going to amount to anything. She had too much of her father in her. She's no loss in the grand scheme of things."

"She was a loss to Michael. She was a loss to Trevor. She was a loss to ... me."

"I am mildly curious how she managed to snag Trevor Gardner," Jessica said. "She was a plain girl and he was a popular kid. He came from money. If I thought they would've lasted I might've tried to come up with a different solution but, let's face it, teen love never survives."

Maddie begged to differ on that opinion. "Your husband may be an animal, but you're the real monster in this. He's sick. You knew what you were doing was wrong. You even apologized to Hayley for what you had to do. I'm kind of curious, though, did you think you killed her at the cabin? When she regained consciousness on the boat, did you give killing her a second time another thought? Do you regret anything you've done?"

"How did you know that Hayley regained consciousness on the boat?" Jessica asked, suspicious. "There's no way you could possibly know that."

There was one way. When she'd touched the rope under the bench ... the rope that Jessica was trying to use to tie Hayley to a rock before dropping her into the water ... she'd seen everything. Worse, though, she'd heard everything. She'd heard every single word mother and daughter exchanged during their final confrontation.

"I know things," Maddie said, seeing no reason to lie. "I know that Hayley and Trevor were planning to go to the police. I'm not sure how you found out, or how you found her at all, but I do know you used your mother's boat and docked behind the Gardner cabin. Did you just decide to check up there on a whim? I'll bet that was it. You just got lucky, didn't you? I guess it doesn't matter.

"You then went inside and confronted Hayley," she continued. "At first Hayley thought you were there to offer support ... she still had illusions abut you being a good mother. Then she thought you were there to talk her out of what she planned on doing. It wasn't until you started strangling her that Hayley realized you were always going to kill her."

"I see those rumors of you being psychic are true," Jessica said, her tone dry. "That's a fun parlor trick you've got there."

Maddie ignored her. "Hayley fought a little, but in the end she was ready to give up. She didn't want to be unhappy. She was tired of it. Her last thought before she passed out was that she was happy because that meant she wouldn't get beaten or raped ever again."

"See, I did her a favor."

"When she woke up on the boat, her first thought was of escape," Maddie said, her eyes glistening with tears. "Even though she gave up that first time, she decided to fight the second time. It was too late, though. She was slow ... and sluggish ... and her mind wasn't firing on all cylinders."

"Her mind was never firing on all cylinders," Jessica said.

"She tried to fight you that second time, but you didn't give her much of a chance," Maddie said. "You strangled her again, and then you dumped her over the side of the boat. You wanted to weigh her down, but it was harder than you thought and the rock came loose, so you just watched until her body floated to the surface. Do you want to know what her final thought was that second time?"

"Not really."

"She thought about Michael," Maddie said, her heart clenching. "She wasn't scared of dying. She was scared that he wouldn't find the strength to go on without her."

"That's what you get when you're best friends with a boy who thinks he's a girl," Jessica said. "He's such a loser. I won't miss seeing his stupid face."

Maddie growled, the sound low and menacing. "You're beyond all redemption."

"I'm not beyond survival, though," Jessica said. "That brings us to a sticky ... conundrum. What am I going to do with you?"

. . .

"WHAT are you doing?" John asked, eyeing Nick as he patted down the front of his jeans.

"I can't find my phone," Nick said. "I thought it was in my pocket."

"Do you need it for something?"

"I want to call Maddie," Nick said. "She was expecting to go to the garage to see the boat. I don't want her wandering around, especially since this storm looks like it's going to be a doozy."

"I'm sure she's smart enough to stay out of the rain," John said. "You got lucky there. She's beautiful and intelligent."

"I'm the luckiest man in the world," Nick agreed, moving to the driver's side of the Explorer and opening the door.

"How long are you going to make me sit here?" Andrew asked, scowling as he tried to get comfortable in the back seat. "My wrists hurt, and I'm starting to lose circulation."

"Good," Nick said, running his hand over the seat. When he saw something black sticking out of the crease he breathed a sigh of relief and yanked his phone out. "Here it is. It must have fallen out of my pocket."

"It's been beeping," Andrew said. "I think someone sent you a text message."

"Thanks," Nick said, scanning the screen. "Maddie texted."

"Text her back and tell her to stay home with Maude," John said. "When we're done processing him we can take them dinner. I haven't seen Maude in a few years. I've always loved her. I want to see the house you're going to be living in, too. I haven't seen that place since I was a teenager."

"That sounds good," Nick said, pressing one of the icons on the phone's screen. When he read Maddie's message, his heart dropped. "I'm going to kill her."

"What's wrong?" John asked, rolling his eyes. "Did you miss your hourly 'I love you' exchange?"

"Get in the truck," Nick ordered, angrily climbing up into the driver's seat.

"What's wrong?" This time John was serious.

"Maddie found the boat," Nick said. "She said she was going to check it out before the storm hit. It's down by the pier, hidden in a bunch of trees."

"Why would she do that?"

"Because she can't help herself," Nick said. "Get in!"

"What are you so worried about?"

"I'm starting to think that Andrew hasn't been lying about not killing Hayley."

"He just admitted to raping and beating her."

"Yeah, but he also admitted his wife is bitter and mean," Nick said. "He said he was scared to hit her. What if Jessica didn't move the boat because she was covering for Andrew? What if she moved the boat because she was covering for herself?"

John was deathly serious now. "Let's go."

"YOU should just let me go," Maddie said. "Adding another murder to your rap sheet isn't going to do you any favors."

"Oh, please," Jessica said, laughing. "No one knows I'm a murderer. There's no way they can prove it. Andrew was the one who beat and raped Hayley. I'm just the long-suffering wife who was terrorized by a madman for two decades.

"When that comes out, everyone is going to be flocking to my side," she continued. "I'm going to be everyone's favorite sympathy case. I'm going to be the most popular woman in town. Heck, the eligible bachelors are going to be lining up to take care of me. Men love taking care of distraught women."

"You're so sick," Maddie said. "Do you really think no one is going to figure this out?"

"Yes. Especially since I have the only person capable of figuring it out right here," Jessica said.

At that exact moment, a long bolt of lightning split the sky, followed by a deafening roar of thunder. The skies opened up and a torrential downpour followed. The storm was here – in more ways than one.

"Nick will figure it out," Maddie said, her hair already damp from the rain. "He's close. He'll figure it out."

"Actually, as soon as he's done mourning you, I'm expecting him to be one of the bachelors lining up to soothe my broken heart," Jessica said, gracing Maddie with an evil smile. "He comes from money, so that will work out. I'm guessing he'll want to help me in my time of need to keep himself busy. After a few months, our grief will lead us to bed and then... ultimately ... to marriage. He's a definite step up from Andrew. He's a little young, but the younger men like a more ... experienced woman these days."

"You're deluded," Maddie said. "Nick knows how to read people. There's no way you'll be able to fool him. Besides, at a certain point your husband is going to tell the truth. You know how sick he is. Do you think he's so stupid he doesn't know how sick you are?"

"That's what I'm counting on," Jessica said. "I'm going to be the lone survivor in this family. Andrew is either going to kill himself tonight – and I've been pushing him toward that decision – or he's going to be arrested. Either way, I'm golden."

"I guess I'm your only loose end," Maddie said, swallowing hard.

"This is true," Jessica said. "The good news is, you came to me. No one knows you're here. Not only that, but you came to me in a storm. That's going to make killing you so much easier. No one is out here to hear you scream."

Jessica reached down her leg and slipped her hand beneath her blue jeans, pulling a knife from a sheath on her calf. Maddie's heart almost stopped at the sight of the blade. It was a hunting knife, all jagged sharp edges, and a deadly tip. It was almost as menacing as Jessica's face. "Now, do you want me to cut your throat or just stab you in the chest? I'm open for suggestions."

## 25. TWENTY-FIVE

"Do you see anything?"

Nick slammed his Explorer into park and peered out the front window. The rain was coming down in a torrent, hitting the pier so hard it bounced. The warmth of the day's sun had heated the boards, so when the cool rain hit a mist began to form.

"There's no one here," John said, following Nick's gaze. "They all got out of the storm. Are you sure that Maddie didn't leave and go back home? Maybe she just forgot to text you."

"That's her car," Nick said, practically choking on the words. "She's here."

John was resigned as he studied the vehicle. "What are you going to do?"

"Find her."

"Have you seen this rain?"

"I don't care about the rain," Nick said. "That's my ... life ... out there. I'm going to find her. You don't have to come. Stay here with him."

"I'm not letting you go out in this alone," John said, irritated. "If you're going out there then I'm coming with you."

"What about me?" Andrew asked, annoyed. "I'm really uncomfortable."

"You're going to sit here and shut up," Nick snapped. "You're a child rapist and a sick bastard. You're the least of my worries." He pushed the door open and hopped out, locking the Explorer with his fob once John joined him on the other side.

"Do you think we should split up?" John asked.

"No," Nick said. "We could cover more ground apart but finding each other again in this is going to be … virtually impossible."

"We'll find her," John said, pushing his hair off his forehead. "She's going to be fine."

"Trouble finds her," Nick said. "It always finds her."

"So do you," John said. "You'll always find her, Nick. That's your strength. This time won't be any different."

Nick could only hope he was right.

**"I'D RATHER** not die," Maddie said, forcing herself to remain calm in the face of Jessica's knife. She nudged over slightly, hoping the darkening sky and nonstop rain would play with Jessica's vision. "You could just let me go. I promise not to tell anyone."

"Oh, we both know that's not true," Jessica said. "You're a do-gooder. Do-gooders can't help themselves from doing good. It's in your nature. I can't let you go. And, the truth is, I really don't want to let you go. I don't like you. I'm looking forward to killing you."

"I'm getting the feeling you don't like anyone," Maddie said, shifting farther along the deck and placing her hands under her rear so she could be ready to push herself to her feet at an opportune moment. The deck of the boat was small, and now it was slick, but Maddie didn't have to outrun Jessica. She just had to get close enough to the side to jump over. The water was choppy, but she wasn't far out. She had a better chance of making it to shore in a storm than surviving Jessica's twisted wrath.

"I like some people," Jessica said. "Nick, for example. He was so worried about my emotional wellbeing this afternoon. He's going to make a great boyfriend."

"Not for you," Maddie spat, her blonde hair dipping across her eye. "I'm not going to just sit here and let you kill me. You know that, right?"

"I didn't expect you to just give in," Jessica said. "You're not a quitter like Hayley. You're still at a disadvantage, though. I'm the one with all the cards."

"Maybe," Maddie said. "That doesn't mean I'm going to go quietly. You should also know I texted Nick and told him where I was – and what I knew – before I got on the boat. He knows what you are." The second part was a lie, but there was no way Jessica could know that.

Jessica narrowed her eyes, tilting her head to the side as she considered Maddie's admission. "I think you're lying. If that was true you would've told me when I first came back to the boat. If that was true your precious Nick would already be here. I don't see him, do you?"

"I guess you'll just have to risk it."

"I guess so."

Maddie was ready when Jessica lunged at her. She was expecting it. She lifted her long leg quickly and placed it in the middle of Jessica's chest as she threw herself in Maddie's direction. Maddie was strong enough to shove Jessica back, the woman teetering to the side and almost toppling over as Maddie jumped to her feet and raced toward the side of the boat.

*Jump!*

It didn't take Jessica long to recover, but Maddie was halfway over the high wall before the crazed woman was on her. Jessica lashed out with the knife, but Maddie was already moving. The tip ripped into the soft tissue of her arm, causing Maddie to scream at the pain. Maddie had momentum on her side, though, and she was dropping toward the angry water below before Jessica could try again.

The water drowned out Maddie's scream as she hit it, but Jessica's angry screech was still loud enough to careen over the angry storm.

"I'm going to kill you!"

. . .

"**DID** you hear that?" John asked, narrowing his eyes as he stared into the storm. "I thought I heard someone on the pier. It sounds like ... footsteps."

"I ... ." Nick broke into a run when he saw a dark figure shuffling toward them, pulling up short when he realized that it wasn't Maddie, disappointment engulfing him.

"What are you doing out here?" David Crowder asked, surprised.

"Have you seen Maddie?" Nick was beside himself.

"She was out here about an hour ago," David said, confused. "She said she was going to find you before the storm hit. I saw her heading toward the parking lot. She's probably home."

"Her car is still here," Nick said. "She never left. She sent me a text that she found a boat that was hidden by some trees. She said she was going to check it out. It's the boat we're looking for. Do you have any idea where it could be?"

David's face was a mask of concern. "I ... the only place I can think of is over there," he said, pointing. "The trees are really thick in that spot, and there's a small area close to deep water where you can kill the engine of a boat, but it's still close enough to the shore to walk to it."

"Let's go," Nick said, clapping John on the shoulder. "That has to be ... ." He broke off when he heard a scream, snapping his head around so he could stare at the dark water. "Did you hear that?"

"It kind of sounded like a scream," John admitted. "I ... I'm not sure, though."

"Maddie," Nick whimpered.

"I'm going to kill you!"

This time all three men jumped into action. They'd definitely heard the threat, muffled as it was across the water. Nick raced to the side of the pier, staring into the water for a source. That's when he saw a bright spot in the middle of the furious water, a head bobbing on the water. "Maddie!"

Maddie turned, her face white as she tried to find Nick in the midst of the tempest's onslaught. "Nicky!"

Nick didn't hesitate. He couldn't. He placed his hands on the side of the pier and vaulted over, dropping to the water beneath and leaving David and John to watch him with astonished looks on their faces. Nick surfaced quickly and immediately started stroking in Maddie's direction. "I'm coming. Swim to me."

"That was ... impressive," David said. "It was like he was one of those heroes in an action movie."

"That's probably the reason he got the girl," John said, turning and running back down the pier. There was no way he was jumping into that water. That didn't mean he didn't have somewhere else to be. He had to find the boat ... and the angry woman on it.

It took Nick longer than he would've liked to close the distance between himself and Maddie, but when he finally saw her up close and personal he couldn't hold back the tears. He grabbed her – harder than he probably should have – and dragged her to him. "Are you okay?"

Maddie's face was ashen, and she was trying to hold the gash on her arm closed despite Nick's insistence on keeping her tight. "She cut my arm. She's crazy. It's Jessica Walker. She's the one who killed Hayley."

"She stabbed you?"

Nick reached for Maddie's arm, his eyes registering the slash in her shirt even though the water was too dark to see how deep the wound delved. "We have to get to shore. This storm is just getting worse. Can you swim?"

"I can do anything with you," Maddie said.

Nick gave her a hard kiss. "We're going to have a long talk about this later. You should never have gotten on that boat."

"I texted you!"

"Later," Nick said. "I need you on land. I can't stop thinking about the last time you were in danger and water was involved. It's ... freaking me out."

"I'm not going to drown, Nicky," Maddie said. "I'm okay."

"Well, that's great, love," Nick said. "We still have to swim to shore and check your arm. And there's still that pesky woman with a knife to worry about."

"Oh, yeah," Maddie said, panting heavily. "She's crazy."

"I figured that out all on my own," Nick said. "Now swim. I'll help you."

**IT TOOK** Nick and Maddie almost five minutes to swim to safety. The waves were so violent that every stroke forward also moved them laterally. By the time they hit the shore they were exhausted.

Maddie tried to keep her footing on solid ground, but her body felt heavy and she stumbled on the sand. She hit her knees before she could gain her full footing. Nick used the last bit of his remaining strength to wrap his arm around her waist and lift her farther up the beach before letting them both collapse in a tangle of limbs and hearts.

Maddie's arms were around his neck within an instant, her body shaking. "I knew you would find me."

"You scared me, Maddie," Nick said, burying his face in her hair. "You need to stop doing that. I'm going to have a heart attack before I hit thirty if you keep this up."

"I thought you would be here," Maddie said. "I texted you. There was no one on the boat. I just wanted to be able to touch a few things before the storm hit. I thought ... I thought Andrew dumped the boat hoping the rain would wash all the evidence away. I didn't realize ... ."

"I didn't realize either," Nick said, rubbing the back of her head. "I didn't figure it out until I arrested Andrew."

"You did?"

"Once we found the boat gone we thought he moved it," Nick said. "He was drunk at the house, though. He admitted to beating and ... um ... ."

"I know he raped Hayley," Maddie said. "I saw ... everything .. when I was on the boat."

Nick cupped the back of her head and kissed her forehead,

keeping her close to him so they could share body heat. "I'm so sorry, love."

"Jessica wasn't sorry," Maddie said, crying openly. "She didn't want anyone to know what was going on so she just decided to kill Hayley. She thought she was worthless ... and stupid ... and beneath her. She knew what her husband was doing as he was doing it. She could've saved Hayley."

"Hayley is out of her reach now," Nick said. "She's safe. She's ... home."

Maddie's chest hitched with a heart-rendering sob. "I want to go home."

"We're going, Mad," Nick said. "I just ... ."

The sound of heavy footsteps in the brush next to beach caught Nick's attention, and he whipped his gun out and leveled it at the dark figure rushing toward them. David jumped back, surprised, and then fixed Nick with a harsh look. "Don't you dare shoot me."

"I thought you were Jessica Walker," Nick said, struggling to his feet. "Come here, Mad. I need to look at your arm."

"Don't worry about that witch," John said, pushing his way through the bushes ten feet away and dragging a struggling Jessica behind him. Her hands were cuffed in front of her, and she was spewing an endless stream of vitriol at John as she pleaded her case.

"I'm innocent, you idiot! My husband made me do it. He's a monster. Why won't you listen to me?"

"You're both monsters," Nick snapped, gingerly running his fingers over Maddie's arm to check the cut. "You should probably get stitches, love."

"I want to go home."

"Well ... you're getting stitches. This won't heal right without them, and you should probably get a tetanus shot while you're there."

"But ... ."

Nick quieted her with a soft kiss. "I'm the boss tonight, Mad. You're getting stitches. John is going to take Jessica and Andrew in and process them, and I'm going to take you to the hospital. Then we're going to pick up some pizza and go home. I'll look at however many paint colors you want me to."

"Really?"

"I just ... I love you, Maddie. Pizza and paint sound just about perfect to me."

Maddie rested her head on Nick's chest, giving in. "I love you, too. Just no onions on the pizza. I have plans for you later."

## 26. TWENTY-SIX

"What are we doing here?"

Maddie lifted her hand to her forehead so she could cut down on the sun's glare and focus on the Winters' family boat.

"Well, this is a boat," Nick teased, lifting the picnic basket he was carrying up so he could hoist it over the side. "You generally use it to cruise around the water."

After six stitches – and an entire pizza – on the night of the big showdown, Maddie and Nick passed out from sheer exhaustion and slept for ten hours. By the time they woke up the next morning Jessica and Andrew were processed and arraigned, both trying to cast aspersions on the other. Neither Nick or Maddie could muster up the energy to go down to the police station to follow up on the case in the intervening hours, instead opting to leave it in John and Kreskin's eager hands. They spent the day in bed, looking over paint colors, and happily shut out the world.

Now, a full twenty-four hours after that, Nick was taking Maddie out for a real boat ride – complete with a picnic. All he cared about was the sun ... and her smile.

"I can't believe you surprised me with this," Maddie said, grinning as she climbed onto the boat. "Are we really getting a whole afternoon alone? That sounds ... amazing."

"We spent all day yesterday together, too," Nick pointed out. "Maude checked in on us a few times, but other than that it was just you and me. Doesn't that count?"

"It does," Maddie said, her eyes sparkling. "It was wonderful. This is better, though."

"It definitely is," Nick said. "I figure we'll go for a ride. Then we can find a place to fish – someplace isolated from everyone else – and maybe do a little ... kissing."

Maddie arched a challenging eyebrow. "Kissing?"

"For starters," Nick said, smirking. "Put the picnic basket below deck, will you? It will spoil if it's not out of the sun."

"Are you going to be bossy today?"

"I'm the captain," Nick said. "You're the first mate."

"Are you going to call me Little Buddy?"

"I'm going to call you the love of my life and leave it at that," Nick said, kissing her lightly. "Hurry up. I have one thing I want to show you before we go off on our own. It won't take long."

Maddie was intrigued, and after stowing their afternoon picnic, she joined Nick on the deck. He maneuvered the boat away from the dock, and before engaging the engine at a higher rate of speed, he tapped the captain's chair he was sitting on. "If you're a good girl, I'll let you steer with me."

Maddie rolled her eyes but joined him, pressing her body against his. She was having just as much fun as he was.

Nick took a leisurely pace on the lake, the boat slowly skimming the water in a "no wake" zone as he kept close to the beach.

"I thought you wanted to take me someplace isolated?" Maddie teased. "I'm not skinny dipping with you when there are so many people around."

"Don't worry about it," Nick said. "I know exactly where we're going ... and you're definitely skinny dipping with me. I see an all-body tan in your future."

"We'll see," Maddie said. She was feeling more adventurous these days, but even she wasn't sure if she was ready to risk someone besides Nick seeing ... everything she had to offer.

"Don't worry, Mad," Nick said, licking the ridge of her ear. "No one will be able to see you. I promise. I don't want to share you with anyone. Trust me. I just want to show you one thing before we head out to my special spot."

"I thought your special spot was at my lake?"

"You're my special spot," Nick said, kissing her jaw as he snuggled closer to her. "It's special whenever I have you in my arms."

"You're being awfully sweet today."

"Today?"

"You're always sweet," Maddie conceded. "I just ... why are we by the pier?"

Nick grinned and killed the engine, letting the boat float as the busy pier denizens swam into view. Nick flipped up his sunglasses and studied the pier for a moment. When he saw who he was looking for he extended his arm and pointed. "I wanted you to see that."

Maddie turned her head, curious, and when she saw what Nick was pointing at she almost wept with joy.

There he was, the curmudgeonly David Crowder in all of his glory. He was on the end of the pier, and he wasn't alone. He had two teenage boys with him – boys who were just as tentative around each other as David was around them.

"It's Trevor and Michael," Maddie said.

"It is," Nick said. "I ran into David when I was picking up sandwiches for our picnic. He told me he was giving fishing lessons to them this afternoon."

"But ... why?"

"He said a certain blonde convinced him that he might be too old to adopt, but he wasn't too old to help kids who were struggling," Nick said, flattening his hands against Maddie's midriff as he leaned forward. "They're trying to become friends and David is trying to help them."

"I don't understand," Maddie said. "I ... I thought they didn't like each other."

"They might not," Nick said. "They both loved the same girl, though. Love can do funny things to people. It can bridge a lot of gaps."

"Do you think ... ?"

"I don't know, Mad," Nick said, sucking in a breath. "It's just a step. I know you're worried about Michael losing his best friend. I just wanted you to see that he's not alone."

Maddie bit her lower lip, considering. "Can I ask you a question?"

"You can ask me anything."

"If it had been us, if I had died when we were in high school, do you think you would have gotten over it?"

"No." Nick answered immediately, no hesitation stilling him.

Maddie turned to him, her eyes shiny. "Are you sure? I want to think Michael is going to be okay."

"Maddie, you moved away and it almost killed me," Nick said. "The only thing that kept me going was that I knew ... deep down ... that you were going to find a way to come back to me. I believed that we would get to ... this."

"How did you know that?"

"I had faith," Nick said. "If you'd died on me ... and just for reference, don't you dare ever die on me ... I wouldn't have ever recovered. That doesn't mean Michael won't have a happy life. No matter how much you identified with Hayley and Michael, they're not you and me."

"I know," Maddie said, turning her attention back to the laughing faces on the pier. "I just think Hayley would have loved this."

"I think, wherever she is, she knows and ... she's okay. The question is: Are you okay?"

"I've never been better," Maddie said, pressing her lips to his softly. "I really haven't."

Nick deepened the kiss, holding her close for a few moments before firing up the boat again. "Good. Now ... how fast can you get naked? I have plans for you once we're away from prying eyes ... and I'm definitely the boss today."

Maddie saluted. "I put myself in your capable hands." Internally, she knew she always would. The sun was the one smiling down on them this day, but Maddie had a feeling Hayley was somewhere watching over them, too.

For today, that was more than enough.

Made in United States
Troutdale, OR
11/09/2023